# Love
# JEANETTE WINTERSON

**VINTAGE** MINIS

Freya,

Happy Holidays

I love you!

Remus x

# Contents

# Oranges Are Not The Only Fruit

IN 1658 THE English clergyman Edward Topsell published a handsome volume of woodcuts called *A History of Four-Footed Beasts and Serpents.*

Some of the creatures were familiar to townspeople and countryfolk alike – the dormouse, the cat, the beaver. Some were fantastical: the sphinx, the lamia, the winged dragon, the mantichora – a lion with a human face. And the unicorn, of course.

Other beasts illustrated by woodcut were ones that are familiar to us now – hippos, rhinos, the Egyptian crocodile, the giraffe – but in the 17<sup>th</sup> century, these creatures had been seen by few – sailors, explorers, convicts, con-men, who described them for gain and pleasure, talked them up in taverns and at fairs, whispered about them in bed late at night, by candlelight, boasted about them for wagers of money and proof of daring. And we all wanted to believe it, because the world was still new, and life was short, and a pair of dragon's wings might come in useful.

So, out of nature and imagination combined, beasts appeared not seen before or since. But they were pictured in a book – and so they came to exist.

**What I want does exist if I dare to find it.**

That's a line from *Oranges Are Not The Only Fruit*, my first novel, published in 1985 when I was twenty-five.

*Oranges* is many things: a coming-of-age story, a coming-out story, a little book of fairy tales, a character called Jeanette who is not me and who is me. A story of religious excess, of working-class life in the north of England, of books and of reading.

And love.

*Oranges* is a quest story. It's the start of a long search for a mythical creature called Love.

I am adopted and that fact has shaped my whole life. At six weeks old I lost the other half of my first love affair – my mother.

So life began with the disappearance of the love object.

My new parents – the Wintersons – found love difficult. They didn't do hugs. My mother was an Old Testament type who believed in fire and brimstone. At the same time the motto of our faith and church was God is Love.

This worked for me because I already had experience of my primary love object being invisible and unreachable.

Solitary by nature and nurture – an only child – I was intense and romantic. School was useless to me, but the library contained all the classics of English literature, and I read them. My roving reading was anchored by Shakespeare at one end and stretched as far as EM Forster at the other end. A few Americans were in there – Henry James, Edith Wharton, Poe, Scott Fitzgerald, Hemingway, Stein. I don't think I read any Europeans back then, other than Gide and Hesse.

Essentially it was 350 years or so of the English imagination, its poetry and prose, that was crucial and formative for me.

And that includes – overshadowing it all, I guess – the King James Bible of 1611, read to me or read by me every single day of my life from babyhood to leaving home at sixteen. That's a lot of Bible.

Literature has only lately been a secular enterprise. Most writers until the 20th century were believers of some kind, or brought up in religious households – the Brontës in their blowy parsonage, John Donne, who gave up sex and writing about it, and became Dean of St Paul's; Laurence Sterne – the amiable author of *Tristram Shandy* – was a vicar. The Romantic poets returned God to Nature. William Blake, like Walt Whitman, saw God in everything.

In the 19<sup>th</sup> century in England and America, doubt was as potent a force as faith. Not to believe was defiant, and like all defiance contained explosive useful creative energy.

So I felt kinship with the underlying beliefs – or struggles with unbelief, tacit or explicit – of the writers I was reading. Growing up today would be a very different experience. Unbelief is the new normal – there's no energy there. And, outside of secularism, the energy of belief we're used to now manifests as fundamentalism, carrying all the hatred and violence of its competing dogmas, but none of the creative release.

The Bible begins with a grand abandonment. Exit from the Garden of Eden. Paradise lost.

Yahweh is an unstable, angry, rejecting parent with a strange idea of love. Later, in the Christian part of the Jewish story, God will allow his son Jesus to be murdered as a human sacrifice to save mankind, doomed by Yahweh in the first place. God is love? Oy veh.

Or is God so in love with his own story that he can't rewrite it?

To me that felt like a failure of imagination. And the failure of love.

I wanted to do better.

You could call it arrogance or you could call it optimism.

———

So when I wrote *Oranges* I chaptered the sections according to the first eight books of the Bible. Not because I thought I was God, or any kind of authority – in fact, the opposite; the thing didn't have to be written on tablets of stone. There was no rigid rulebook. No last word.

I had understood something – I could change the story.

Could I?

Writing is an attempt to make a world. I was telling myself the story of myself. In *Oranges* I became a fictional character trying to understand love – and coming to understand that, without love, nothing can be understood.

It was first love, awakening love, love as separation, love as sleepless nights and broken hearts. Love as trial by fire. The fearfulness of love. And it was love between women. There wasn't much written about that back then.

Love between women became, for some readers, a way of trying to categorise the book – to lock it into a smaller space than it occupied. I have always been clear – I am a writer whose emotional interest is forwarded towards women, and whose sexual interest usually is. That is important, but it isn't the reason I write, nor does it preoccupy me.

Heterosexual choice is allowed to be the background of a writer's life; its wallpaper. So is maleness. And whiteness. Step out of that and you will be called a feminist writer, a lesbian writer, a gay writer, a woman writer. A black writer. You will never be called a heterosexual writer or a male writer or a white writer. Those signifiers are absorbed into the single word 'writer'.

It is changing. I have been part of the change. And glad to be. It matters to stand up politically for what you believe in. It matters to carry into the mainstream what the mainstream has tried to marginalise.

But writing is more than content. More than the stories we tell. Literature is an engagement with our deepest selves, a shaping of a language to talk about who we are – away from clichés and approximations, away from generalisations and half-truths. And oddly, literature is a way, at last, of not having to talk about anything. The moment that you put the book down. The moment you stare into space. A knowing that is beyond ordinary knowing. Resolution? Or peace? Or illumination? To pass through language back into silence. We start with silence, and we return to silence, but without language to guide us we cannot return there because

Words are the part of silence that can be spoken.

*Oranges* is about transgressive love – love between young women – and young women who wanted their love to include sex. Why would you not want love to include sex?

*Oranges* is about absences as well as inclusions; the absence of family love. What do you do if your parents don't know how to love you, and if you don't know how to love your parents?

And overarching the story is God's love – whatever that is. Invisible love – problematic and potent.

And I suppose those demonstrations of love were what I was trying to follow.

Love. Loss. Struggle. Loneliness. Abandonment. Separation. Faithfulness. Rejection. The natural world as an ally. Home as a place to leave behind. The search for meaning.

And could meaning be found through love?

Meaning.
Love.

What do those words mean, comets that they are, their tails stretched with stars? Their tales stretched with stars?

I was trying to trace light that had long left its source.

The story of my life starts there. Or is it here?

LIKE MOST PEOPLE I lived for a long time with my mother and father. My father liked to watch the wrestling. My mother liked to wrestle; it didn't matter what. She was in the white corner and that was that.

She hung out the largest sheets on the windiest days. She wanted the Mormons to knock on the door. At election time in a Labour mill town, my mother put a picture of the Conservative candidate in the window.

My mother had never heard of mixed feelings. There were friends and there were enemies.

Enemies were:     The Devil (in his many forms)
                  Next Door
                  Sex (in its many forms)
                  Slugs

Friends were:     God
                  Our dog
                  Auntie Madge
                  The Novels of Charlotte Brontë
                  Slug pellets

And me, at first. I had been brought in to join her in a tag match against the Rest of the World. She had a mysterious attitude towards the begetting of children; it wasn't that she couldn't do it, more that she didn't want to do it. She was very bitter about the Virgin Mary getting there first. So she did the next best thing and arranged for a foundling. That was me.

This is both me and not me. *Oranges* isn't autobiography or confessional. Part fiction, part fact is what life is. The stories we tell are all cover versions.

———

MY MOTHER AND I walked on towards the hill that stood at the top of our street. We lived in a town stolen from the valleys, a huddled place full of chimneys and little shops and back-to-back houses with no gardens. The hills surrounded us, and our own pushed out into the Pennines, broken here and there with a farm or a relic from the war. There used to be a lot of old tanks but the council took them away. The town was a fat blot, and the streets spread back from it into the green, steadily upwards. Our house was almost at the top of a long stretchy street. A flag-stone street with a cobbled road. Climb to the top of the hill and look down and you can see everything, just like Jesus on the pinnacle, except it's not very tempting. Over to the right, there's the viaduct, and behind the viaduct, Ellison's Tenement, where we have the fair once a year. I was allowed to go there on condition that I brought back a tub of black peas for my mother. Black peas look like rabbit droppings and they come in a thin gravy made of stock and gypsy mush ... Once when I was collecting the black peas, about to go home, the old woman took hold of my hand. I thought she was going to bite me. She looked at my palm and laughed a bit. 'You'll never marry,' she said, 'not you, and you'll never be still.'

She didn't take any money for the peas, and she told me to run home fast. I ran and ran, trying to understand what she meant. I hadn't thought about getting married anyway. There were two women I knew who didn't have husbands at all; they were old though, as old as my mother. They ran a newspaper shop, and sometimes, on a Wednesday, they gave me a banana bar with my comic. I liked them a lot and I talked about them a lot to my mother. One day, they asked me if I'd like to go to the seaside with them. I ran home, gabbled it out, and was busy emptying my money box to buy a new bucket and spade, when my mother said firmly, and forever, no. I couldn't understand why not, and she wouldn't explain. She didn't even let me go back to say I couldn't go. Then she cancelled my comic and told me to collect it from another shop, further away. I was sorry about that. I never got a banana bar from Grimsby's.

A couple of weeks later I heard her telling Mrs White about it. She said they dealt in unnatural passions. I thought she meant they put chemicals in their sweets.

Does sex begin with a sense of transgression?

As long as I have known them my mother has gone to bed at four and my father has got up at five

Does love survive the loss of physical intimacy?

IT WAS SPRING, the ground still had traces of snow, and I was about to be married. My dress was pure white and I had a golden crown. As I walked up the aisle the crown got heavier and heavier and the dress more and more difficult to walk in. I thought everyone would point at me, but no one noticed.

Somehow I made it to the altar. The priest was very fat and kept getting fatter, like bubblegum you blow. Finally we came to the moment, 'You may kiss the bride.' My new husband turned to me, and here were a number of possibilities. Sometimes he was blind, sometimes a pig, sometimes my mother, sometimes the man from the post office, and once, just a suit of clothes with nothing inside. I told my mother about it, and she said it was because I ate sardines for supper. The next night I ate sausages, but I still had the dream.

There was a woman in our street who told us all she had married a pig. I asked her why she did it, and she said, 'You never know until it's too late.'

Exactly.

No doubt that woman had discovered in life what I had discovered in my dreams. She had unwittingly married a pig.

I kept watch on him after that. It was hard to tell he was a pig. He was clever, but his eyes were close together, and his skin bright pink. I tried to imagine him without his clothes on. Horrid.

Other men I knew weren't much better.

The man who ran the post office was bald and shiny with hands too fat for the sweet jars. He called me poppet, which my mother said was nice. He gave me sweets too, which was an improvement.

One day he had a new sort.

'Sweet hearts for a sweet heart,' he said and laughed. That day I had almost strangled my dog with rage, and been dragged from the house by a desperate mother. Sweet I was not. But I was a little girl, ergo, I was sweet, and here were sweets to prove it. I looked in the bag. Yellow and pink and sky-blue and orange, and all of them heart-shaped and all of them said things like,

Maureen 4 Ken,

Jack 'n' Jill, True.

On the way home I crunched at the Maureen 4 Kens. I was confused. Everyone always said you found the right man.

My mother said it, which was confusing.

My auntie said it, which was even more confusing.

The man in the post office sold it on sweets.

But there was the problem of the woman married to the pig, and the spotty boy who took girls down backs, and my dream.

That afternoon I went to the library. I went the long way, so as to miss the couples. They made funny noises that sounded painful, and the girls were always squashed against the wall. In the library I felt better; words you could trust and look at till you understood them, they couldn't change half way through a sentence like people, so it was easier to spot a lie. I found a book of fairy tales, and read one called 'Beauty and the Beast'.

In this story, a beautiful young woman finds herself the forfeit of a bad bargain made by her father. As a result, she has to marry an ugly beast, or dishonour her family forever. Because she is good, she obeys. On her wedding night she gets into bed with the beast, and feeling pity that everything should be so ugly, gives it a little kiss. Immediately, the beast is transformed into a handsome young prince, and they both live happily ever after.

I wondered if the woman married to a pig had read this story. She must have been awfully disappointed if she had. And what about my Uncle Bill? He was horrible, and hairy, and looking at the picture, transformed princes aren't meant to be hairy at all.

Slowly I closed the book. It was clear that I had stumbled on a terrible conspiracy.

There are women in the world.

There are men in the world.

And there are beasts.

What do you do if you marry a beast?

Kissing them didn't always help. And beasts are crafty. They disguise themselves like you and I.

Like the wolf in 'Little Red Riding Hood'.

Why had no one told me? Did that mean no one else knew?

Did that mean that all over the globe, in all innocence, women were marrying beasts?

I reassured myself as best I could. The minister was a man, but he wore a skirt, so that made him special. There must be others, but were there enough? That was the worry. There were a lot of women, and most of them got married. If they couldn't marry each other, and I didn't think they could, because of having babies, some of them would inevitably have to marry beasts.

My own family had done quite badly, I thought.

If only there was some way of telling, then we could operate a ration system. It wasn't fair that a whole street should be full of beasts.

That night, we had to go to my auntie's to play Beetle. She was in the team at church, and needed to practise. As she dealt the cards, I asked her, 'Why are so many men really beasts?'

She laughed. 'You're too young for that.'

My uncle had overheard. He came over to me, and put his face close.

'You wouldn't love us any other way,' he said, and rubbed his spiky chin against my face. I hated him.

'Leave off, Bill,' my auntie pushed him away. 'Don't worry, love,' she soothed, 'you'll get used to it. When I married, I laughed for a week, cried for a month, and settled down for life. It's different, that's all, they have their little ways.' I looked at my uncle, who was now sunk in the pools coupon.

'You hurt me,' I accused.

'No I didn't,' he grinned. 'It was just a bit of love.'

'That's what you always say,' my auntie retorted, 'now shut up or go out.'

He slunk off. I half expected him to have a tail.

She spread the cards. 'There's time enough for you to get a boy.'

'I don't think I want one.'

'There's what we want,' she said, putting down a jack, 'and there's what we get, remember that.'

'You hurt me.

'No I didn't. It was just a bit of love.'

Was she trying to tell me she knew about the beasts? I got very depressed and started putting the Beetle legs on the wrong way round, and generally making a mess. Eventually my auntie stood up and sighed. 'You might as well go home,' she said.

I went to fetch my mother, who was in the parlour listening to Johnny Cash.

'Come on, we're finished.'

Slowly she put on her coat, and picked up her little Bible, the travel-size one. We set off together down the street.

'I've got to talk to you, have you got time?'

'Yes,' she said, 'let's have an orange.'

I tried to explain my dream, and the beast theory, and how much I hated Uncle Bill. All the time my mother walked along humming 'What a Friend We Have in Jesus', and peeling me an orange. She stopped peeling and I stopped talking about the same time. I had one last question.

'Why did you marry my dad?'

She looked at me closely.

'Don't be silly.'

'I'm not being silly.'

'We had to have something for you, and besides, he's a good man, though I know he's not one to push himself. But don't you worry, you're dedicated to the Lord, I put you down for missionary school as soon as we got you. Remember Jane Eyre and St John Rivers.' A faraway look came into her eye.

I did remember, but what my mother didn't know was

that I now knew she had rewritten the ending. *Jane Eyre* was her favourite non-Bible book, and she read it to me over and over again, when I was very small. I couldn't read it, but I knew where the pages turned. Later, literate and curious, I had decided to read it for myself. A sort of nostalgic pilgrimage. I found out, that dreadful day in a back corner of the library, that Jane doesn't marry St John at all, that she goes back to Mr Rochester. It was like the day I discovered my adoption papers while searching for a pack of playing cards. I have never since played cards, and I have never since read *Jane Eyre*.

We continued our walk in silence. She thought I was satisfied, but I was wondering about her, and wondering where I would go to find out what I wanted to know.

When it was washday I hid in the dustbin to hear what the women said. Nellie came out with her bit of rope and strung it up nail to nail across the back alley. She waved to Doreen who was struggling up the hill with her shopping, offering her a cup of tea and a talk. Each Wednesday Doreen queued up at the butcher's for the special offer mince. It always put her in a bad mood because she was a member of the Labour party and believed in equal shares and equal rights. She started to tell Nellie about the woman in front buying steak. Nellie shook her head which was small and tufted, and said it had been hard for her too since Bert died.

'Bert,' spat Doreen, 'he were dead ten years before they laid him out.' Then she offered Nellie a wine gum.

'Well I don't like to speak ill of the dead,' said Nellie uneasily, 'you never know.'

Doreen snorted and squatted painfully on the back step. Her skirt was too tight, but she always pretended it had shrunk.

'What about speaking ill of the living? My Frank's up to no good.'

Nellie took a deep breath and another wine gum. She asked if it was the woman who served pie and peas in the pub; Doreen didn't know, but now that she thought of it that would explain why he always smelled of gravy when he came home late.

'You should never have married him,' scolded Nellie.

'I didn't know what he was when I married him, did I?' And she told Nellie about the war and how her dad had liked him, and how it seemed sensible. 'I should have guessed though, what kind of a man comes round to court you and ends up drinking with your dad instead? I used to sit all done up playing whist with his mother and one of her friends.'

'Did he not take you anywhere then?'

'Oh yes,' said Doreen, 'we used to go down the dog track every Saturday afternoon.'

The two of them sat in silence for a while then Doreen went on, 'Course the children helped. I ignored him for fifteen years.'

'Still,' Nellie reassured her, 'you're not as bad as Hilda across the road, her one drinks every penny, and she daren't go to the police.'

'If mine touched me I'd have him put away,' said Doreen grimly.

'Would you?'

Doreen paused and scratched in the dirt with her shoe.

'Let's have a smoke,' offered Nellie, 'and you tell me about Jane.'

Jane was Doreen's daughter, just turned seventeen and very studious.

'If she don't get a boyfriend folks will talk. She spends all her time at that Susan's doing her homework, or so she tells me.'

Nellie thought that Jane might be seeing a boy on the quiet, pretending to be at Susan's. Doreen shook her head. 'She's there all right, I check with Susan's mother. If they're not careful folk will think they're like them two at the paper shop.'

'I like them two,' said Nellie firmly, 'and who's to say they do anything?'

'Mrs Fergeson across saw them getting a new bed, a double bed.'

'Well what does that prove? Me and Bert had one bed but we did nothing in it.'

Doreen said that was all very well, but two women were different.

Different from what? I wondered from inside the dustbin.

'Well your Jane can go to university and move away, she's clever.'

'Frank won't put up with that, he wants grandchildren, and if I don't get a move on there'll be no dinner for him and he'll be back with pie and peas in the pub. I don't want to give him an excuse.'

She struggled to her feet as Nellie started to peg out the washing. When it was safe, I crept out of the dustbin, as confused as ever and covered in soot.

It was a good thing I was destined to become a missionary. For some time after this I put aside the problem of men and concentrated on reading the Bible. Eventually, I thought, I'll fall in love like everybody else. Then some years later, quite by mistake, I did.

'By mistake . . .' Does love always happen by chance? That's one of the questions of this first book of mine and many that followed. I still haven't found the answer but the question has become more problematic to me. I like the idea of free will but the ancients knew a thing or two about Fate.

I WOULDN'T HAVE noticed Melanie if I hadn't gone round the other side of the stall to look at the aquarium.

She was boning kippers on a big marble slab. She used a thin stained knife, throwing the gut into a tin bucket. The clean fish she laid on greaseproof paper. Every fourth fish had a sprig of parsley.

'I'd like to do that,' I said.

She smiled and carried on.

'Do you like doing it?'

Still she said nothing, so I slid, as discreetly as a person in a pink plastic mac can, to the other side of the tank. I couldn't see very well because of the hood over my eyes.

'Can I have some fish-bait?' I said.

She looked up, and I noticed that her eyes were a lovely grey, like the cat Next Door.

'I'm not supposed to have friends at work.'

'But I'm not your friend.'

'No, but they'll think you are.'

'Well ... I might as well be then ...'

What follows in *Oranges* is the unfolding of this relationship – how it moves from an unexpected friendship to an unexpected love affair. The girls I am writing about are not savvy, not sophisticated. There was no internet back then. They don't know anyone like themselves. They are both going to church and reading the Bible and they feel happy there, and happy together. And then the thing deepens, because the body can't lie.

WHEN I REACHED MELANIE'S it was getting dark. I had to cut through the churchyard to get to her. Sometimes I'd steal her a bunch of flowers from the new graves. She was always pleased but I never told her where they came from. She asked me if I wanted to stay overnight because her mum was away and she didn't like being in the house on her own. I said I'd ring a neighbour, and after a lot of trouble finally got an agreement from my mother, who had to be fetched from her lettuces. We read the Bible as usual, and we told each other how glad we were that the Lord had brought us together. She stroked my head for a long time, and then we hugged, and it felt like drowning. Then I was frightened but couldn't stop. There was something crawling in my belly. I had an octopus inside me ...

'Do you think this is Unnatural Passions?'

HERE IS A TABLE set at feast and the guests are arguing about the best recipe for goose. A tremor shakes the chandelier, dropping tiny flakes of plaster into the sherbet. The guests look up, more in interest than alarm. It's cold in here. So cold. The women suffer most. Their shoulders bared and white like hard-boiled eggs. Outside, under the snow, the river sleeps embalmed. These are the elect, and in the hall, an army sleeps on straw.

Outside, a rush of torches.

Laughter drifts through the hall. The elect have always been this way.

Getting old. Dying. Starting again. Not noticing.

Father and Son. Father and Son.

It has always been this way. Nothing can intrude.

Father, Son, and Holy Ghost.

Outside, the rebels storm the Winter Palace.

Love, the naturaliser of everything artificial, and at the same time the ultimate artifice, the elaborate construct, the mind's narrative of the body's desire. Love, the destroyer.

The change in Jeanette (me and not me) is noticed by her mother, who at first concludes that her daughter has fallen for a good-looking lad at church. As the Chief of the Sex Police, Mother feels the time is right for the story of Pierre . . .

'THERE'S A BOY at church I think you're keen on.'

'What?' I said, completely mystified.

She meant Graham, a newish convert, who'd moved over to our town from Stockport. I was teaching him to play the guitar, and trying to make him understand the importance of regular Bible study.

'It's time,' she went on, very solemn, 'that I told you about Pierre and how I nearly came to a bad end.' Then she poured us both a cup of tea and opened a packet of Royal Scot. I was enthralled.

'It's not something I'm proud of, and I'll only say it once.'

My mother had been headstrong, and had got a job teaching in Paris, which was a very daring thing to do at the time. She had lived off the Rue St Germain, eaten croissants and lived a clean life. She wasn't with the Lord then, but she had high standards. Then, one sunny day, without warning, she had been walking towards the river when she met Pierre, or rather Pierre had jumped from his bicycle, offered her his onions, and named her the most beautiful woman he had ever seen.

'Naturally, I was flattered.'

They exchanged addresses, and began to court one another. It was then that my mother experienced a feeling she had never known before: a fizzing and a buzzing and a certain giddiness. Not only with Pierre, but anywhere, at any time.

'Well, I thought it must be love.'

But this puzzled her because Pierre wasn't very clever, and didn't have much to say, except to exclaim how beautiful she was. Perhaps he was handsome? But no, looking in the magazines, she realised he wasn't that either. But the feeling wouldn't go away. Then, on a quiet night, after a quiet supper, Pierre had seized her and begged her to stay with him that night. The fizzing began, and as he clutched her to him, she felt sure she would never love another, and yes she would stay and after that, they would marry.

'Lord forgive me, but I did it.'

My mother stopped, overcome with emotion. I begged her to finish the story, proffering the Royal Scots.

'The worst is still to come.'

I speculated on the worst, while she chewed her biscuit. Perhaps I wasn't a child of God at all, but the daughter of a Frenchman.

A couple of days afterward, my mother had gone to see the doctor in a fit of guilty anxiety. She lay on the couch while the doctor prodded her stomach and chest, asking if she ever felt giddy, or fizzy in the belly. My mother coyly explained that she was in love, and that she often felt strange, but that wasn't the reason for her visit.

'You may well be in love,' said the doctor, 'but you also have a stomach ulcer.'

Imagine my mother's horror. She had given away her all for an ailment. She took the tablets, followed the diet, and refused Pierre's entreaties to visit her. Needless to say, the next time they met, and again by chance, she felt nothing, nothing at all, and shortly fled the country to avoid him.

'Then am I . . . ?' I began.

'There was no issue,' she said quickly.

For a few moments we sat silent, then:

'So just you take care, what you think is the heart might well be another organ.' It might, Mother, it might, I thought. She got up and told me to go and find something to do. I decided to go and see Melanie, but just as I reached the door she called me back with a word of warning.

'Don't let anyone touch you Down There,' and she pointed to somewhere at the level of her apron pocket.

'No Mother,' I said meekly, and fled.


I TRACED THE OUTLINE of her marvellous bones and the triangle of muscle in her stomach. What is it about intimacy that makes it so disturbing?


Love ends, of course. I mean, the love affair ends badly, because the church calls it a sin and the girls are separated. Melanie believes her love for Jeanette was a perversion, and she's glad to start dating boys, and eventually to marry. For Jeanette, things are more complicated. She can't lie about her feelings.

There's a further relationship with another girl – eventually discovered, and that's it – she's out of house and home, living what kind of a patched-together life she can until she leaves for university.

During her first Christmas holiday she returns to find her mother has bought an electronic organ and built a CB radio to broadcast the gospel to the Heathen – mainly the Heathen living in Manchester.

I MISS GOD. I miss the company of someone loyal. I don't think of God as my betrayer. I miss God who was my friend. I don't know if God exists but I know that if God is your emotional role model, few human relationships will match up. I have an idea that it might be possible. I thought once it had become possible, and that glimpse of something has sent me wandering, trying to find the balance between earth and sky.

I can't settle. I want someone who is fierce and who will love me unto death and know that love is as strong as death and be on my side for ever and ever. I want someone who will destroy and be destroyed by me. There are many forms of love and affection; some people can spend their whole lives together without knowing each other's names. Naming is difficult and time-consuming; it concerns essences and it means power.

On the wild nights, who can call you home? Only the one who knows your name.

Romantic love has been diluted into paperback form and has sold thousands and millions of copies. Somewhere it is still in the original, written on tablets of stone ...

The unknownness of my needs frightens me. I do not know how huge they are or how high they are. I only know that they are not being met ...

One thing I am certain of – I do not want to be betrayed, but that's quite hard to say, casually, at the beginning of a relationship. There are different kinds of infidelity but betrayal is betrayal wherever you find it. By betrayal I mean promising to be on your side, then being on someone else's.

STANDING ON THE SIDE of the hill where it slopes into the quarry, it's possible to see where Melanie used to live. I met her by accident during the second year I didn't live at home. She was pushing a pram. She had been serene to the point of bovine before; now she was nearly vegetable. I kept looking at her wondering how we had ever had a relationship, yet when she first left me I thought I had blood poisoning. I couldn't forget her. Now she seemed to have forgotten everything. I wanted to shake her. Pull off all my clothes in the middle of the street and yell REMEMBER THIS BODY?

Time is a great deadener. People forget, get bored, grow old, go away.

She said that not much had happened between us

anyway, historically speaking. But history is a string full of knots, the best you can do is admire it and maybe knot it up some more. History is a hammock for swinging and a game for playing. A cat's cradle.

She said those sorts of feelings were dead – the feelings she once had for me. There is a seductiveness about dead things. You can ill treat, alter, and recolour what's dead – it won't complain. Then she laughed and said we probably saw what had happened very differently anyway. She laughed again – she said that the way I saw it would make a good story, her version was just the history, the nothing-at-all facts. She said she hoped I hadn't kept any letters, silly to hang onto old things that had no meaning. As though letters and photos made it more real, more dangerous.

I told her I didn't need letters and photos to remember what had happened. Then she looked vague and started to discuss the weather and the roadworks and the soaring price of baby food.

SHE ASKED ME what I was doing and I longed to say I was sacrificing infants on top of Pendle Hill. Anything to make her angry. But she was happy. They had stopped eating meat and she was pregnant again. She had even started writing to my mother.

It was getting dark as I came down the hill, swirls of snow sticking to my face. I thought about the dog and was sad for her death, for my death, for all the inevitable dying that comes with change. There's no choice that doesn't mean a loss. But the dog was buried in the clean earth and the things I had buried were exhuming themselves; clammy fears and dangerous thoughts and the shadows I had put away for a more convenient time. I could not put them away for ever; there is always a day of reckoning. But not all dark places need light. I have to remember that.

I DO HAVE to remember that – all these years later. Not all dark places need light.

# The Passion

LOVE AS THE night-haunter, the blood-hunter, the body's rack, antagonist of commonsense.

Love as the space between utility and despair.

Love as the enemy of ease.

When I wrote *The Passion* I was magnificently and recklessly in love with a married woman twenty years older than me. To deal with the feelings this invoked – and I mean invoked (it felt like a kind of conjuring) – I did what writers have always done and transposed the situation.

I went back in time to the Napoleonic Wars and wrote about Henri, a young soldier, about his strange meeting with a woman with webbed feet called Villanelle, about her entanglement with both Henri and a mysterious older woman bored by her marriage. And I set it in Venice, a city I visited for the first time after I had written the book.

I saw no reason to go before I was writing the book – or while I was writing it – it was a novel, not a travel guide, and the Venice of the 1800s was gone. I couldn't visit it. What I could do was invent it.

It's not that art imitates life. Creativity releases life from both time and gravity. Events can be reversed, endings change, the weight that bears down on all that we do is lifted.

*The Passion* is a good story. It's got love, sex, murder, friendship, war, politics and characters we care about. TV and movies have brought us into the age of story-telling like never before. Advertising and market-manipulation are all about the story. And no one can resist a story – we're hard-wired to sit round that camp fire and hear what the story-teller has to say.

For me, though, and the texts that interested me, story-telling was a magic carpet to elsewhere. The elsewhere wasn't the story, it was further on – it was where the story might lead.

The last line of *The Passion,* and yes, it does get printed on T-shirts a lot, is this:

I'm telling you stories. Trust me

Why should we trust fictions in a post-truth world?

When I wrote *The Passion* we weren't in a post-truth world – or we thought we weren't. It was the year after deregulation of the markets, the beginning of the economy on steroids that would lead, twenty years later, to the biggest financial crash in history. So everything we were being told, everything we were experiencing, had no truth in it, if truth is lasting, real, dependable, verifiable.

But we didn't know that. Thatcher and Reagan ruled the world. Love your neighbour as yourself had been replaced with Love yourself. The social contract was dead.

Thirty years later, thinking about *The Passion* and about fiction versus lying, I realise all the obvious things about invention as a way of getting at a deeper truth, and lying as a way of avoiding any truth at all or, worse, creating a nightmare world where nothing is as it seems, where nothing can be depended upon – we know human minds can't cope with that, and then we instinctively cling to the 'strong man', who is usually the biggest liar of the lot.

All that is clear enough.

What's less clear is this question of the story itself being a means rather than an end. A map rather than a destination.

And that's what stories have in common with Love.

Love is a means, not an end. Love is a map, not a destination. That's why there is no such thing as 'they all lived happily ever after'.

That's why Act V of the Shakespeare comedies is often so uncomfortable. We know that, in the mirth and resolution, what lies ahead is the start of another play, another journey.

Love is the visible corner of a folded map.

So my commitment to story-telling, like my commitment to love, is a commitment to discomfort, not security. To adventure, not satisfaction. To possibilities, not answers.

And you'll note, because it is so obvious that it needs saying, that lies are always offered as answers.

Brexit. Trump. Border control. Make your own list.

Truth is a questioning place.

Stories are full of questions. What if? What is? Who am I? Who are you? What do I believe? Why do I believe it?

We ask these questions in other ways – of course we do, politically, philosophically, spiritually. We address them head-on.

And that's the difference, I guess, because, as Freud worked out at the start of the 20th century, human beings cannot always, or even optimally, address the big, the dark, the difficult, the shameful, the guilty, the criminal, the crazy head-on. We have to go sideways, downwards, away from without running away. We use a proxy or an avatar. And that's what stories let happen.

———

When we are in love we have the feeling of being understood. The feeling of things being simultaneously settled and disturbed. Hands and voices rummage through us.

We are known while remaining private.
We are held while remaining free.

I'm telling you stories. Trust me

Here, Villanelle, dressed as a boy, meets the mysterious woman for the second time:

NOVEMBER IN VENICE is the beginning of the catarrh season. Catarrh is part of our heritage like St Mark's. Long ago, when the Council of Three ruled in mysterious ways, any traitor or hapless one done away with was usually announced to have died of catarrh. In this way, no one was embarrassed. It's the fog that rolls in from the lagoon and hides one end of the Piazza from another that brings on our hateful congestion. It rains too, mournfully and quietly, and the boatmen sit under sodden rags and stare helplessly into the canals. Such weather drives away the foreigners and that's the only good thing that can be said of it. Even the brilliant water-gate at the Fenice turns grey.

On an afternoon when the Casino didn't want me and I didn't want myself, I went to Florian's to drink and gaze at the Square. It's a fulfilling pastime.

I had been sitting perhaps an hour when I had the feeling of being watched. There was no one near me, but there was someone behind a screen a little way off. I let my mind retreat again. What did it matter? We are always watching or watched. The waiter came over to me with a packet in his hand.

I opened it. It was an earring. It was the pair.

And she stood before me and I realised I was dressed as I had been that night because I was waiting to work. My hand went to my lip.

'You shaved it off,' she said.

I smiled. I couldn't speak.

She invited me to dine with her the following evening and I took her address and accepted.

In the Casino that night I tried to decide what to do. She thought I was a young man. I was not. Should I go to see her as myself and joke about the mistake and leave gracefully? My heart shrivelled at this thought. To lose her again so soon. And what was myself? Was this breeches and boots self any less real than my garters? What was it about me that interested her?

You play, you win. You play, you lose. You play.

I was careful to steal enough to buy a bottle of the best champagne.

Lovers are not at their best when it matters. Mouths dry up, palms sweat, conversation flags and all the time the heart is threatening to fly from the body once and for all. Lovers have been known to have heart attacks. Lovers drink too much from nervousness and cannot perform. They eat too little and faint during their fervently wished consummation. They do not stroke the favoured cat and their face-paint comes loose. This is not all. Whatever you have set store by, your dress, your dinner, your poetry, will go wrong.

Her house was gracious, standing on a quiet waterway, fashionable but not vulgar. The drawing-room, enormous with great windows at either end and a fireplace that would have suited and idle wolfhound. It was simply furnished; an oval table and a *chaise-longue*. A few Chinese ornaments that she liked to collect when the ships came through. She had also a strange assortment of dead insects mounted in cases on the wall. I had never seen such things before and wondered about this enthusiasm.

She stood close to me as she took me through the house, pointing out certain pictures and books. Her hand guided my elbow at the stairs and when we sat down to eat she did not arrange us formally but put me beside her, the bottle in between.

We talked about the opera and the theatre and the visitors and the weather and ourselves. I told her that my real father had been a boatman and she laughed and asked could it be true that we had webbed feet?

'Of course,' I said and she laughed the more at this joke.

We had eaten. The bottle was empty. She said she had married late in life, had not expected to marry at all being stubborn and of independent means. Her husband dealt in rare books and manuscripts form the east. Ancient maps that showed the lairs of griffins and the haunts of whales. Treasure maps that claimed to know the whereabouts of the Holy Grail. He was a quiet and cultured man of whom she was fond.

He was away.

We had eaten, the bottle was empty. There was nothing more that could be said without strain or repetition. I had been with her more than five hours already and it was time to leave. As we stood up and she moved to get something I stretched out my arm, that was all, and she turned back into my arms so that my hands were on her shoulder blades and hers along my spine. We stayed thus for a few moments until I had courage enough to kiss her neck very lightly. She did not pull away. I grew bolder and kissed her mouth, biting a little at the lower lip.

She kissed me.

'I can't make love to you,' she said.

Relief and despair.

'But I can kiss you.'

And so, from the first, we separated our pleasure. She lay on the rug and I lay at right angles to her so that only our lips might meet. Kissing in this way is the strangest of distractions. The greedy body that clamours for satisfaction is forced to content itself with a single sensation and, just as the blind hear more acutely and the deaf can feel the grass grow, so the mouth becomes the focus of love and all things pass through it and are re-defined. It is a sweet and precise torture.

# Sexing the Cherry

WHEN JORDAN WAS a baby he sat on top of me much as a fly rests on a hill of dung and I nourished him as a hill of dung nourishes a fly. And when he had eaten his fill he left me.

Jordan ...

I should have named him after a stagnant pond and then I could have kept him, but I named him after a river, and in the flood-tide he slipped away.

*Sexing the Cherry* is set in the reign of Charles the First, and I suppose it's an historical novel, except that the past is always history, and the past is happening every minute.

I wasn't trying to reproduce a historical period, or ventriloquise the dead. I was using the past as a place to situate what interested me.

I have never believed that to be relevant we have to

write about our own time and place. Literature isn't documentary. Using the past is a way of escaping the clutter of now.

*Sexing the Cherry* is my third novel, published when I was twenty-nine. It's the story of a giantess called the Dog-Woman, who lives on the banks of the River Thames, breeding hounds. She adopts a boy called Jordan, fished out of the river, and this is their fierce unrequited-love story – love between mother and son – love that never quite joins them together. They are both loners, and in an essential sense they remain alone.

Love is baffling. Love can leave us lonelier than we were without love. Love, like a planet that appears in the sky, dazzling and unreachable.

But loneliness is not the same thing as emotional defeat.

WHEN JORDAN WAS a boy he made paper boats and floated them on the river. From this he learned how the wind affects a sail but he never learned how love affects the heart. His patience was exceeded only by his hope. He spent days and nights with his bits of wood salvaged from chicken crates, and any piece of paper he could steal became a sail. I used to watch him standing in the mud or lying face down, his nose almost in the current, his hand steadying the boat and then letting it go straight into the wind. Letting go hours of himself.

When the time came he did the same with his heart. He didn't believe in shipwreck.

And he came home to me with his boats broken and his face streaked with tears and we sat with our lamp and mended what we could and the next day was the first day all over again. But when he lost his heart there was no one to sit with him. He was alone.

The novel previous to this one, *The Passion*, also has a young man in it, a soldier called Henri, similarly baffled by love. I see no reason to write in your own gender, unless there is a reason to do so. I see no reason to read as your own gender either. Fictional characters are the original avatars for writer and reader alike. In this place of freedom we can choose who we want to be. And we can find a spectrum of feeling, experience, sexuality, even anger or murder, not available in daily life.

But *Sexing the Cherry* belongs to the Dog-Woman. I think she must be a reading of my adoptive mother, Mrs Winterson, who never wanted to be a nobody, and liked dogs. She was also very large – and I am not. So there is size in *Sexing the Cherry*, a novel that is in some ways a fairy tale, and contains twelve little fairy tales. And in fairy tales size is often approximate and unstable. Genies and giants, little people and shape-shifters.

The twelve fairy tales are the stories of the Twelve Dancing Princesses. I liked that story when I was a child, but

I used to wonder about the lives of the girls. Who were they? When I realised I was a writer, I realised I could find out.

Here's one of the stories:

You may have heard of Rapunzel.

Against the wishes of her family, who can best be described by their passion for collecting miniature dolls, she went to live in a tower with an older woman.

Her family were so incensed by her refusal to marry the prince next door that they vilified the couple, calling one a witch and the other a little girl. Not content with names, they ceaselessly tried to break into the tower, so much so that the happy pair had to seal up any entrance that was not on a level with the sky. The lover got in by climbing up Rapunzel's hair, and Rapunzel got in by nailing a wig to the floor and shinning up the tresses flung out of the window. Both of them could have used a ladder, but they were in love.

One day the prince, who had always liked to borrow his mother's frocks, dressed up as Rapunzel's lover and dragged himself into the tower. Once inside he tied her up and waited for the wicked witch to arrive. The moment she leaped through the window, bringing their dinner for the evening, the prince hit her over the head and threw her out again. Then he carried Rapunzel down the rope he had brought with him and forced her to watch while he blinded her broken lover in a field of thorns.

After that they lived happily ever after, of course.

As for me, my body healed, though my eyes never did, and eventually I was found by my sisters, who had come in their various ways to live on this estate.

My own husband?

Oh well, the first time I kissed him he turned into a frog.

There he is, just by your foot. His name's Anton.

Back then, British writers like Angela Carter, Michele Roberts and Sara Maitland were breaking into the sealed and locked rooms of fairy stories, and re-telling them, not as PC versions, or feminist versions, necessarily, but claiming the right to re-write, which is part of the feminist proposal. Text, starting with the Bible, has always been a way of claiming knowledge and tradition. Text has been a class-war weapon to keep people in their place. And a gendered weapon too; who is allowed to read? Who is allowed to write? What is the canon? What is literature? And who claims it?

I was conscious of myself as a working-class woman writing. So I was happy to do a pirate raid on the treasure chest of the past. Anyway, it is only when stories are written down that they become codified – myths, legends, fairy tales existed, and still do, in multiple oral versions. The written version is propositional. Isn't it?

So why not propose something different?

———

But to return to the Dog-Woman. She is a lost soul. She will never be found. Her lostness is part of her glory and she glories in it. She is a magnificent misfit. She howls on the banks of the Thames beside her dogs. She barges through life, alternately terrorising and mourning. And in my version of history, she is responsible for the Great Fire of London.

Why not? Just burn it down.

But it is love, not revenge, that occupies her thoughts.

WHAT IS LOVE?

On the morning after our arrival at Wimbledon I awoke in a pool of philosophic thought, though comforted by Jordan's regular breathing and the snorts of my thirty dogs.

I am too huge for love. No one, male or female, has ever dared to approach me. They are afraid to scale mountains.

I wonder about love because the parson says that only God can truly love us and the rest is lust and selfishness.

In church, there are carvings of a man with his member swollen out like a marrow, rutting a woman whose teats swish the ground like a cow before milking. She has her eyes closed and he looks up to Heaven, and neither of them notice the grass is on fire.

The parson had these carvings done especially so that we could contemplate our sin and where it must lead.

There are women too, hot with lust, their mouths sucking at each other, and men grasping one another the way you would a cattle prod.

We file past every Sunday to humble ourselves and stay clean for another week, but I have noticed a bulge here and there where all should be quiet and God-like.

For myself, the love I've known has come from my dogs, who care nothing for how I look, and from Jordan, who says that though I am as wide and muddy as the river that is his namesake, so am I too his kin. As for the rest of this sinning world, they treat me well enough for my knowledge and pass me by when they can.

I breed boarhounds as my father did before me and as I hoped Jordan would do after me. But he would not stay. His head was stuffed with stories of other continents where men have their faces in their chests and some hop on one foot defying the weight of nature.

These hoppers cover a mile at a bound and desire no sustenance other than tree-bark. It is well known that their companions are serpents, the very beast that drove us all from Paradise and makes us still to sin. These beasts are so wily that if they hear the notes of a snake-charmer they lay one ear to the earth and stopper up the other with their tails. Would I could save myself from sin by stoppering up my ears with a tail or any manner of thing.

I am a sinner, not in body but in mind. I know what love sounds like because I have heard it through the wall, but I do not know what it feels like. What can it be like, two bodies slippery as eels on a mud-flat, panting like dogs after a pig?

I fell in love once, if love be that cruelty which takes us

straight to the gates of Paradise only to remind us they are closed for ever.

There was a boy who used to come by with a coatful of things to sell. Beads and ribbons hung on the inside and his pockets were crammed with fruit knives and handkerchiefs and buckles and bright thread. He had a face that made me glad.

I used to get up an hour early and comb my hair, which normally I would do only at Christmas-time in honour of our Saviour. I decked myself in my best clothes like a bullock at a fair, but none of this made him notice me and I felt my heart shrivel to the size of a pea. Whenever he turned his back to leave I always stretched out my hand to hold him a moment, but his shoulder blades were too sharp to touch. I drew his image in the dirt by my bed and named all my mother's chickens after him.

Eventually I decided that true love must be clean love and I boiled myself a cake of soap ...

I hate to wash, for it exposes the skin to contamination. I follow the habit of King James, who only ever washed his fingertips and yet was pure in heart enough to give us the Bible in good English.

I hate to wash, but knowing it to be a symptom of love I was not surprised to find myself creeping towards the pump in the dead of night like a ghoul to a tomb. I had determined to cleanse all of my clothes, my underclothes and myself. I did this in one passage by plying at the pump handle, first with my right arm and washing my left self, then with my left arm and washing my right self. When I was so drenched that to wring any part of me left a puddle at my feet I waited outside the baker's until she began her work and sat myself by the ovens until morning. I had a white coating from the flour, but that served to make my swarthy skin more fair.

In this new state I presented myself to my loved one, who graced me with all of his teeth at once and swore that if only he could reach my mouth he would kiss me there and then. I swept him from his feet and said, 'Kiss me now,' and closed my eyes for the delight. I kept them closed for some five minutes and then, opening them to see what had happened, I saw that he had fainted dead away. I carried him to the pump that had last seen my devotion and doused him good and hard, until he came to, wriggling like a trapped fox, and begged me let him down.

'What is it?' I cried. 'Is it love for me that affects you so?'

'No,' he said. 'It is terror.'

I saw him a few months later in another part of town with a pretty jade on his arm and his face as bright as ever.

Here she is again:

IN THE DARK and in the water I weigh nothing at all. I have no vanity but I would enjoy the consolation of a lover's face. After my only excursion into love I resolved never to make a fool of myself again. I was offered a job in a whore-house but I turned it down on account of my frailty of heart.

Surely such to-ing and fro-ing as must go on night and day weakens the heart and inclines it to love? Not directly, you understand, but indirectly, for lust without romantic matter must be wearisome after a time. I asked a girl at the Spitalfields house about it and she told me she hates her lovers by-the-hour but still longs for someone to come in a coach and feed her on mince pies.

Where do they come from, these insubstantial dreams?

As for Jordan, he has not my common sense and will no doubt follow his dreams to the end of the world and then fall straight off.

I cannot school him in love, having no experience, but I can school him in its lack and perhaps persuade him that there are worse things than loneliness.

A man accosted me on our way to Wimbledon and asked me if I should like to see him.

'I see you well enough, sir,' I replied.

'Not all of me,' said he, and unbuttoned himself to show a thing much like a pea-pod.

'Touch it and it will grow,' he assured me. I did so, and indeed it did grow to look more like a cucumber.

'Wondrous, wondrous, wondrous,' he swooned, though I could see no good reason for swooning.

'Put it in your mouth,' he said. 'Yes, as you would a delicious thing to eat.'

I like to broaden my mind when I can and I did as he suggested, swallowing it up entirely and biting it off with a snap.

As I did so my eager fellow increased his swooning to the point of fainting away, and I, feeling both astonished by his rapture and disgusted by the leathery thing filling up my mouth, spat out what I had not eaten and gave it to one of my dogs.

The whore from Spitalfields had told me that men like to be consumed in the mouth, but it still seems to me a reckless act, for the member must take some time to grow again. None the less their bodies are their own, and I who know nothing of them must take instruction humbly, and if a man asks me to do the same again I'm sure I shall, though for myself I felt nothing.

In copulation, an act where the woman has a more pleasurable part, the member comes away in the great tunnel and creeps into the womb where it splits open after a time like a runner bean and deposits a little mannikin to grow in the rich soil. At least, so I am told by women who have become pregnant and must know their husbands' members as well as I do my own dogs.

When Jordan is older I will tell him what I know about the human body and urge him to be careful of his member. And yet it is not that part of him I fear for; it is his heart. His heart.

# Written on the Body

WHY IS THE measure of love loss?

That's the opening line of *Written on the Body*.

What do we do about love? So impossible, so essential, a drug, a lifesaver, the killer, and the cure.

I'm talking here about romantic love, sexual love, only. I say 'only' but you know what I mean.

In *Oranges* I had thought about love between young women, and in *The Passion* between women and between men and women. Now I wondered what would happen if we didn't know, weren't told, the gender of the narrator. How would we read love if it didn't come with the usual signifiers?

There's a beloved – Louise – who is married. Triangles are more interesting than straight lines – for dramatic, if not domestic, purposes. Her lover is not named and we know almost nothing about him or her. What we know is the unfolding story of their love affair.

> Written on the body is a secret code only visible in cer-
> tain light

I am bored by binaries. Are you? I think of male and female as subsets of a totality. Not quite like Plato's hermaphrodites – but forced apart by nurture, not nature, most of us having more of the other in us than social norms allow. What does it mean to love as a man? What does it mean to love as a woman? And does the character of our love change if our own gender, or the gender of our lover, changes?

Why is gender so defining in our culture?

I'm writing this in 2017. A lot has changed since 1992 – but quite a lot hasn't changed at all. Men and women are still judged by different sexual standards. Women who wear trousers are fine. Men who wear skirts or make-up are stared at in the street.

Women have been 'allowed' to express their masculine side – mainly because we want women in the workforce, and work is still, somewhere deep down, associated with what men do. If you don't believe that look at the comments from blue-collar Trump voters wanting 'real' jobs for 'real' men.

Men have fared less well in expressing their feminine side – they are often a little awkward about house-husbanding, taking paternity leave, or even crying. Feminism gives me hope here, because feminism was, and is, an agenda for change for both women and men. And as

Grayson Perry has often said, when talking about his alter ego, Clare, is there really a 'masculine' and a 'feminine' at all?

Younger people are more accepting of bisexuality or intersexuality, and see more flexibility in what we think of as gender norms, but it would be optimistic to say there is no prejudice, no fear, no judgement.

I wanted to undo assumptions. Assumptions about male and female. Assumptions about desire.

Fiction is a set of possibilities. Those possibilities prompt us towards other beginnings, alternative endings, because to some extent we write the book alongside the author, and we often would prefer a different ending. I was aware of this, and so I left the space for it to happen – and, in fact, for the novel to begin again.

Here's the end:

THIS IS WHERE the story starts, in this threadbare room. The walls are exploding. The windows have turned into telescopes. Moon and stars are magnified in this room. The sun hangs over the mantelpiece. I stretch out my hands and reach the corners of the world. The world is bundled up in this room. We can take the world with us when we go and sling the sun under your arm. Hurry now, it's getting late. I don't know if this is a happy ending, but here we are let loose in open fields.

I realise that all my books have second chances in them –
some taken and some not. And *Written on the Body* is
my first shadow-working of Shakespeare's *The Winter's
Tale*.

By which I mean loss and its consequences.

That Louise is miraculously alive and in the room at the
end of the story is a direct reference to what happens at
the end of *The Winter's Tale*. We always hope we can return
the dead. That time can unhappen. That we won't be left
alone, staring at the emptiness.

We wish we could undo what we did . . .

None of us lives without loss. Or regret. But none of us
need live without imagination. We can learn to see past
ourselves.

To write a book without a gendered narrator has caused a
few problems. There are problems of translation in those
languages that use gendered verbs and nouns – my advice
was always to keep switching from masculine to feminine,
so that the language itself became a player in the upset of
assumption. I don't think too many publishers took that
advice. A pity!

And then there were problems from readers – wanting
to know, needing to know, which was interesting and
revealing. And then, where the book is taught in class,
there have been tutors who prefer biography over imagination and assume that because I am a woman the narrator
must be a woman. That's just sad!

And there have been gay readers who want this to be a gay love story – and it can be if that is what you want, and I have no problem with that – but it doesn't have to be one.

The great thing about gay culture is how it has challenged heterosexual culture at so many levels. At its simplest, men can now wear pink shirts. At its most profound are questions of sexual identity – the range of sexual expression, the drive not to label anyone according to their sexual choice or destiny.

To judge each other less.

There's a line in the book – 'It's the clichés that cause the trouble. To live beyond cliché is not so easy.'

Fiction helps us to try.

This extract comes early in the novel when the narrator, trying to escape from a rackety past and a nightmare affair with a woman called Bathsheba, has settled with a nice girl who isn't interesting any more. Sex with Louise has already happened.

I PHONED A friend whose advice was to play the sailor and run a wife in every port. If I told Jacqueline I'd ruin everything and for what? If I told Jacqueline I'd hurt her beyond healing and did I have that right? Probably I had nothing more than dog-fever for two weeks and I could get it out of my system and come home to my kennel.

Good sense. Common sense. Good dog.

What does it say in the tea-leaves? Nothing but a capital L.

When Jacqueline came home I kissed her and said, 'I wish you didn't smell of the Zoo.'

She looked surprised. 'I can't help it. Zoos are smelly places.'

She went immediately to run a bath. I gave her a drink thinking how I disliked her clothes and the way she switched on the radio as soon as she got in.

Grimly I began to prepare our dinner. What would we do this evening? I felt like a bandit who hides a gun in his mouth. If I spoke I would reveal everything. Better not to speak. Eat, smile, make space for Jacqueline. Surely that was right?

The phone rang. I skidded to get it, closing the bedroom door behind me.

It was Louise.

'Come over tomorrow,' she said. 'There's something I want to tell you.'

'Louise, if it's to do with today, I can't ... you see, I've decided I can't. That is I couldn't because, well what if, you know ...'

The phone clicked and went dead. I stared at it the way Lauren Bacall does in those films with Humphrey Bogart. What I need now is a car with a running board and a pair of fog lights. I could be with you in ten minutes Louise. The trouble is that all I've got is a Mini belonging to my girlfriend.

We were eating our spaghetti. I thought, As long as I don't say her name I'll be all right. I started a game with myself, counting out on the cynical clock face the extent of my success. What am I? I feel like a kid in the examination room faced with a paper I can't complete. Let the clock go faster. Let me get out of here. At 9 o'clock I told Jacqueline I was exhausted. She reached over and took my hand. I felt nothing. And then there we were in our pyjamas side by side and my lips were sealed and my cheeks must have been swelling out like a gerbil's because my mouth was full of Louise.

I don't have to tell you where I went the next day.

During the night I had a lurid dream about an ex-girlfriend of mine who had been heavily into papier-mâché. It had started as a hobby; and who shall object to a few buckets of flour and water and a roll of chicken wire? I'm a liberal and I believe in free expression. I went to her house one day and poking out of the letter-box just at crotch level was the head of a yellow and green serpent. Not a real one but livid enough with a red tongue and silver foil teeth. I hesitated to ring the bell. Hesitated because to reach the bell meant pushing my private parts right into the head of the snake. I held a little dialogue with myself.

ME:   Don't be silly. It's a joke.

I:      What do you mean it's a joke? It's lethal.

ME:   Those teeth aren't real.

I:      They don't have to be real to be painful.

ME:   What will she think of you if you stand here all
        night?

I:      What does she think of me anyway? What kind of
        a girl aims a snake at your genitals?

ME:   A fun-loving girl.

I:      Ha Ha.

The door flew open and Amy stood on the mat. She was
wearing a kaftan and a long string of beads. 'It won't hurt
you,' she said. 'It's for the postman. He's been bothering me.'

'I don't think it's going to frighten him,' I said. 'It's only a
toy snake. It didn't frighten me.'

'You've nothing to be frightened of,' she said. 'It's got a
rat-trap in the jaw.' She disappeared inside while I stood
hovering on the step holding my bottle of Beaujolais
Nouveau. She returned with a leek and shoved it in the
snake's mouth. There was a terrible clatter and the bottom
half of the leek fell limply on to the mat. 'Bring it in with you,
will you?' she said. 'We're eating it later.'

I awoke sweating and chilled. Jacqueline slept peacefully
beside me, the light was leaking through the old curtains.
Muffled in my dressing gown, I went into the garden, glad of
the wetness suddenly beneath my feet. The air was clean

with a hint of warmth and the sky had pink clawmarks pulled through it. There was an urban pleasure in knowing that I was the only one breathing the air. The relentless in-out-in-out of millions of lungs depresses me. There are too many of us on this planet and it's beginning to show. My neighbour's blinds were down. What were their dreams and nightmares? How different it would be to see them now, slack in the jaw, bodies open. We might be able to say something truthful to one another instead of the usual rolled-up Goodmornings.

I went to look at my sunflowers, growing steadily, sure that the sun would be there for them, fulfilling themselves in the proper way at the proper time. Very few people ever manage what nature manages without effort and mostly without fail. We don't know who we are or how to function, much less how to bloom. Blind nature. Homo sapiens. Who's kidding whom?

So what am I going to do? I asked Robin on the wall. Robins are very faithful creatures who mate with the same mate year by year. I love the brave red shield on their breast and the determined way they follow the spade in search of worms. There am I doing all the digging and there's little Robin making off with the worm. Homo sapiens. Blind Nature.

I don't feel wise. Why is it that human beings are allowed to grow up without the necessary apparatus to make sound ethical decisions?

The facts of my case are not unusual:

1  I have fallen in love with a woman who is married.
2  She has fallen in love with me.
3  I am committed to someone else.
4  How shall I know whether Louise is what I must
   do or must avoid?

The church could tell me, my friends have tried to help me, I could take the stoic course and run from temptation or I could put up sail and tack into this gathering wind.

For the first time in my life, I want to do the right thing more than I want to get my own way. I suppose I owe that to Bathsheba ...

I remember her visiting my house soon after she had returned from a six-week trip to South Africa. Before she had gone, I had given her an ultimatum: Him or me. Her eyes, which very often filled with tears of self-pity, had reproached me for yet another lover's half-nelson. I forced her to it and of course she made the decision for him. All right. Six weeks. I felt like the girl in the story of Rumpelstiltskin who is given a cellar full of straw to weave into gold by the following morning. All I had ever got from Bathsheba were bales of straw but when she was with me I believed that they were promises carved in precious stone. So I had to face up to the waste and the mess and I worked hard to sweep the chaff away. Then she came in, unrepentant, her memory gone as ever, wondering why I hadn't returned her trunk calls or written poste restante.

'I meant what I said.'

She sat in silence for about fifteen minutes while I glued

the legs back on a kitchen chair. Then she asked me if I was seeing anybody else. I said I was, briefly, vaguely, hopefully.

She nodded and turned to go. When she got to the door she said, 'I intended to tell you before we left but I forgot.'

I looked at her, sudden and sharp. I hated that 'we'.

'Yes,' she went on, 'Uriah got NSU from a woman he slept with in New York. He slept with her to punish me of course. But he didn't tell me and the doctor thinks I have it too. I've been taking the antibiotics so it's probably all right. That is, you're probably all right. You ought to check though.'

I came at her with the leg of the chair. I wanted to run it straight across her perfectly made-up face.

'You shit.'

'Don't say that.'

'You told me you weren't having sex with him anymore.'

'I thought it was unfair. I didn't want to shatter what little sexual confidence he might have left.'

'I suppose that's why you've never bothered to tell him that he doesn't know how to make you come.'

She didn't answer. She was crying now. It was like blood in the water to me. I circled her.

'How long is it you've been married? The perfect public marriage. Ten years, twelve? And you don't ask him to put his head between your legs because you think he'll find it distasteful. Let's hear it for sexual confidence.'

'Stop it,' she said, pushing me away. 'I have to go home.'

'It must be seven o'clock. That's your home-time, isn't it?

That's why you used to leave the practice early so that you could get a quick fuck for an hour and a half and then smooth yourself down to say, "Hello, darling," and cook dinner.'

'You let me come,' she said.

'Yes, I did, when you were bleeding, when you were sick, again and again I made you come.'

'I didn't mean that. I meant we did it together. You wanted me there.'

'I wanted you everywhere and the pathetic thing is I still do.'

She looked at me. 'Drive me home, will you?'

# Art and Lies

FROM A DISTANCE only the light is visible; a speeding gleaming horizontal angel, trumpet out on a hard bend. The note bells the beauty of the stretching train that pulls the light in a long gold thread. It catches in the wheels, it flashes on the doors that open and close, that open and close, in commuter rhythm.

On the overcoats, briefcases, brooches, the light snags in rough-cut stones that stay unpolished. The man is busy. He hasn't time to see the light that burns his clothes and illuminates his face. The light pouring down his shoulders in biblical excess. His book is a plate of glass.

*Art and Lies* is a fragmented set of narratives. Three stories, Handel, Picasso, Sappho, but not the composer, not the painter, and somewhat the poet. Nobody finds love or comes near to doing so. Love is unreadable, untranslatable. Love as bafflement. Love as regret.

I don't know why the last line is, 'It was not too late.' I don't feel this book has hope in it.

I think I was lost when I was writing it and this was not a ball of string in the minotaur's labyrinth. I think I was the minotaur.

They are on the same train, Handel, Picasso, Sappho, fleeing a city where anything anyone would want to keep has fled already.

There is a question at the heart of this book:
How shall I live?

I think I was asking myself and getting no answers. But sometimes you have to get lost – both as a writer and as a reader. Sometimes only the question can be asked and the answer is somewhere in the distance – maybe a long way in the distance.

What I know is that life is distance learning. The next thing is out of reach. We reach it. The next thing is out of reach. We reach it.

IT HAPPENED, LATE one afternoon, when David arose from his couch and was walking upon the roof of his house, that he saw from the roof a woman bathing, and the woman was very beautiful. And David sent and inquired about this woman. And one said, 'Is not this Bathsheba, the daughter of Eliam, the wife of Uriah the Hittite?' So David sent messengers and took her; and she came to him and he lay with her. Then she returned to her house. And the woman conceived and she sent and told David, 'I am with child.'

So David sent word to Joab saying, 'Send me Uriah the Hittite.' Then David said to Uriah, 'Go down to your house and wash your feet.' And Uriah went out of the king's house and there followed him a present from the king. But Uriah slept at the door of the king's house with all the servants of his lord and did not go down to his house.

David said, 'Have you not come from a journey? Why did you not go down to your house?'

Uriah said to David, 'The ark, and Israel, and Judah dwell in booths and my lord Joab and the servants of my lord are camping in the open field; shall I then go to my house to eat and to drink and to lie with my wife? As you live and as your soul lives, I will not do this thing.' Then David said to Uriah, 'Remain here today also and tomorrow I will let you depart.' So Uriah remained in Jerusalem that day and the next. And David invited him and he ate in his presence and drank so that he made him drunk; and in the evening he went out to lie on his couch with the servants of his lord but he did not go down to his house. In the morning David wrote a letter to Joab and sent it by the hand of Uriah, 'Set Uriah in the forefront of the hardest fighting and then draw back from him that he may be struck down and die.' And as Joab was besieging the city he assigned Uriah to the place where he knew there were valiant men, and some of the servants of David fell. Uriah the Hittite was slain also.

When the wife of Uriah heard that Uriah her husband was dead she made lamentation for her husband. And when the mourning was over David sent and brought her to his house and she became his wife and bore him a son. But the thing that David had done displeased the Lord.

And the Lord sent Nathan to David. He came to him and said to him, 'There were two men in a certain city, the one rich and the other poor. The rich man had very many flocks and herds but the poor man had nothing but one little ewe lamb which he had bought. And he brought it up and it grew up with him and with his children; it used to eat of his morsel and drink of his cup and lie in his bosom and it was like a daughter to him. Now there came a traveller to the rich man and he was unwilling to take one of his own flock or herd to prepare for the wayfarer, but he took the poor man's lamb and prepared it for the man who had come to him.'

Then David's anger was greatly kindled against the man and he said to Nathan, 'As the Lord lives the man who has done this deserves to die and he shall restore the lamb fourfold, because he did this thing and because he had no pity.'

Nathan said to David, 'You are the man.'

(2 Samuel, 11 and 12:1–7)

'Because he had no pity.' The punishable sin is not lust, not even adultery, the sin is not to do with sex at all. It is a failure of feeling. Not an excess of passion but a lack of compassion.

I am a Sexualist. In flagrante delicto. The end-stop of the universe. Say my name and you say sex. Say my name and you say white sand under a white sky white trammel of my thighs.

Let me net you. Roll up roll up for the naked lady, tuppence a peep. Tup me? Oh no, I do the tupping in this show. I'm the horned god, the thrusting phallus, the spar and mainsail of this giddy vessel. All aboard for the Fantasy Cruise from Mitylene to Merrie England by way of Rome and passing through La Belle France. How long will it take? Not much more than two and a half thousand years of dirty fun and all at my own expense.

Am I making any sense? No? Here's a clue: Very Famous Men have written about me, including Alexander Pope (Englishman 1688–1744 Occupation: Poet) and Charles Baudelaire (Frenchman 1821–67 Occupation: Poet). What more can a girl ask?

I have a lot of questions, not least, WHAT HAVE YOU DONE WITH MY POEMS? When I turn the pages of my manuscripts my fingers crumble the paper, the paper breaks up in burnt folds, the paper colours my palms yellow. I look like a nicotine junkie. I can no longer read my own writing. It isn't surprising that so many of you have chosen to read between the lines when the lines themselves have become more mutilated than a Saturday night whore.

I've had to do that too; go down on the cocks of Very
Famous Men, and that has put me in a position to tell you
a trade secret: Their dose tastes just the same as anyone
else's. I'm no gourmet but I know a bucket of semolina
when I've got my head in it. You can lead a whorse to water
but you can't make her drink. My advice? Don't swallow it.
Spit the little hopefuls down the sink and let them wriggle
up the drain. No, I'm not hard-hearted but I have better
things to do with my stomach lining. And I have another
question: When did he last go down on you?

So many men have got off on me. Large men, small men,
bald men, fat men. Men with a hose like a fire-fighter, men
with nothing but a confectioner's nozzle. Here they come,
poking through the history books, telling you all about me.

I was born on an island. Can you see the marble beach
and the glass sea? Both are lies. The white sand damp-
veined is warm underfoot. The sea that softly reflects the
hull will splinter it soon. What appears is not what is. I love
the deception of sand and sea.

'A Deceiver.' 'A notorious seducer of women.' 'A Venom.'
'A God.' 'The Tenth Muse.' It is the job of a poet to name
things, blasphemy when the things rise up to name the poet.
The praise is no better than the blame. My own words have
been lost amongst theirs.

Examine this statement: 'A woman cannot be a poet' Dr
Samuel Johnson (Englishman 1709–84 Occupation: Language Fixer and Big Mouth.) What then shall I give up? My
poetry or my womanhood? Rest assured I shall have to let

go of one if I am to keep hold of the other. In the end the choice has not been mine to make. Others have made it for me.

In the old days I was a great poet but a bad girl. See Plato (Greek 427–347 BC Occupation: Philosopher), then, Ovid came along in the first century AD and tried to clean up my reputation with a proper tragic romance. Me, who could have had any woman in history, fell for a baggy-trousered bus conductor with the kind of below-the-waist equipment funsters put on seaside postcards for a joke. Fuck him? I couldn't even find him. He said I must have bad eyesight, I said it must be because of all those poems I was writing, late at night with only a tallow candle to keep me company. He said I should give it up, it was ruining our sex life.

# The World and Other Places

IN THIS NIGHT-SOAKED bed with you it is courage for the day I seek. Courage that when the light comes I will turn towards it. Nothing could be simpler. Nothing could be harder.

In this night-covered world with you I hope to find what I'm looking for; a clue, a map, a bird flying south. And in the morning we will get dressed together and go.

There's a line in Virginia Woolf's essay 'On Being Ill', where she says, 'We do not know our own souls, let alone the souls of others.'

This soul-searching is what writing does/is. Drilling down through the layered accumulations of convention, cliché, fear, neglect, prejudice, hatred, tradition, good and bad, buried dreams and forgotten desires. Is the soul there at all? Yours? Mine? And is there any better way of knowing our own soul than through the souls of others?

———

I believe that fiction, long or short, can work on many levels all at once. The story, of course. The characters. Their lives.

A time that isn't our own – if the text is from the past, or if it is set in the past. Feelings evoked we might not otherwise feel. We expect fiction to deliver other places, other people.

But when we go deeper?

It hasn't been too fashionable to talk about the soul. We live in a material world. Religion is discredited as superstition or, worse, fundamentalism. Spirituality, even when detached from religion, looks a bit hippy, woolly, vague; a comfort-zone for those who can't quite manage life as a biological and chemical accident with miraculous consequences.

Already my language gives me away: miraculous consequences.

If you believe that life has an inside as well as an outside, then how can we recognise and protect that inner life? Develop it?

That has to be the job of art. Nothing works better as a tool for going deeper.

I am a writer because I want to go deeper.

I am on a quest. Is everything a quest story? Probably.

I look at the short fictions and I find the same preoccupations as in my longer work.

There's a story in *The World and Other Places* called 'The

Three Friends'. It's a little fairy story type thing – do you search for riches? Power? Sex?

Or that which cannot be found?

Does that seem like a hopeless quest? A journey for masochists only?

Maybe. But every time I get an answer it leads me to another question. That's all I know. The infinity of space.

The world . . . yes. But what about the other places?

There's a line in *The Powerbook*, 'When I was born I became the visible corner of a folded map.'

That's the journey. That's the unfolding. That's what the stories are.

THE BOAT IN the water . . .

I want to push further; to find the hidden cove, the little bay of delight that fear prevents. Sometimes I want to ride out the storm for no better reason than I need the storm. And if I die, I die. That's the gamble, the game. I cannot protect myself although I can take precautions. Society can protect me least of all. It does it by limiting my freedom. Freedom or protection? What kind of choice is that?

In the boat on the water, these things are clear.

# The Powerbook

LOVING YOU IS LIKE lifting a heavy stone. It would be easier not to do it and I'm not sure why I am doing it. It takes all my strength and all my determination and I said I wouldn't love someone again like this.

Is there any sense in loving someone you can only wake up to by chance?

*The Powerbook* was a millennium novel, published in the wi-fi optimism of a new century.

Writers are all multiple personalities – that's why we're hard to live with – and the internet seemed to offer that playing shape-shifting of character, time, place, that is the core of fiction-making.

So I imagined a story where two people would play with each other online – inventing masks and costumes for themselves – it's a theatrical book. Unfolding their personal stories through a series of make-believe stories. And

**Loving you is like lifting a heavy stone. It would be easier not to do it and I'm not sure why I am doing it**

meeting in real life, to discover the entanglement of their actual and virtual worlds.

Yes. It's a love story.

THE STORIES WE sit up late to hear are love stories. It seems that we cannot know enough about this riddle of our lives. We go back and back to the same scenes, the same words, trying to scrape out the meaning. Nothing could be more familiar than love. Nothing else eludes us so completely.

In one strange scene a feral self-taught chemist finds his daughter moving among the dim-lit laboratory jars. She finds one labelled with a heart and a dagger. She picks it up, curious, afraid. Suddenly her father's whiskery face is right behind her.

'NEVER TOUCH THAT JAR! Never! If that gets loose, we're finished.'

'What's in it?'

'Love! There's love in that jar ...'

And so I discovered that love is a hazardous liquid.

There's no particular century to that scene. It's gothic but it could be now. I like moving about in time. Only in the outside world are we constrained by time. Our inner lives move freely between past, present and future, and we don't remember chronologically; memories apart in time sit side by side emotionally. As we get older our lives begin to form a pattern, not a straight line.

Fiction has real strengths here. As in the fairy tales, we can fall asleep and a hundred years flies past, or the actions of a lifetime can be compressed into a single day. In fiction, time can accelerate or slow down. That makes it satisfying because everyone knows that, whatever the clock says, an hour with someone you love passes far faster than an hour of boredom in a place you hate.

And I like history. I like writing about the past. The past is not the present as costume drama. Dropping our minds into the past is an underwater experience. We're weightless, floating in an element not our own. The light is blurry, the sights strange. And that experience is both liberating and unsettling.

As writers and readers we can go where we want to. For me, some fast cutting between one time and another – dropping in a story that's out of the main action, for instance – gives a breathing space and a different view.

*The Powerbook* is packed with stories – it's like having different windows open on your screen.

The writer of these stories, Ali, or Alix – because X marks the spot – will write you anything you like, provided you are prepared to enter the story as yourself and leave it as someone else.

> To avoid discovery I stay on the run. To discover things
> for myself, I stay on the run

And I suppose this book has a motto. I took it from Harold
Bloom's translation of the Jewish Blessing:

MORE LIFE INTO A TIME WITHOUT BOUNDARIES

I like that.

The extract below is a real meeting (I think) after a
series of virtual encounters:

THE EVENING WAS cooling. She and I had walked without
speaking, back over the Pont Neuf, to a little triangle of
grass and birch trees set on all sides with small restaurants.
I like to eat here. Someone once called it 'the sex of Paris'.

I was angry with myself. The afternoon had been an
anticipation – I don't know what for – I do know what for,
but I would have been glad and disappointed if nothing had
started to happen. If we had gone to the restaurant as
planned, and the rest had stayed as a memory whose truth-
fulness is not in the detail.

The trouble is that in imagination anything can be perfect. Downloaded into real life, it was messy. She was messy.
I was messy. I blamed myself. I had wanted to be caught.

We slowed down. She spoke.

'You're angry with me.'

'This is the place – Paul's.'

'I said too much too soon.'

'The décor hasn't changed since the 1930s.'

'I don't hold you cheap.'

'The women who serve wear white aprons and won't speak English.'

'I just want to hold you.'

She took me in her arms and I was so angry I could have struck her, and at the bottom of my anger, conducting it, was a copper coil of desire.

'And I want to kiss you.'

A man was exercising two Dalmatians under the trees. Spots ran in front of my eyes.

'Kiss you here and here.'

The man threw them two red tennis balls and the dogs ran for the balls and fetched them back – black and white and red, black and white and red.

This feels like a grainy movie – the black dresses and white aprons of the matrons moving inside the lighted window of Paul's. Your black jeans and white shirt. The night wrapping round you like a sweater. Your arms wrapped round me. Two Dalmatians.

Yes, this is black and white. The outlines are clear. I must turn away. Why don't I?

In my mouth there is a red ball of desire.

'These tiny hairs on your neck ...'

Fetch. My heart returns to me what I turn away. I am my own master but not always master of myself. This woman wants to be ...

'Your lover.'

We went inside. I ordered artichoke vinaigrette and slices of duck with haricots verts. You had pea soup and smoked eel. I could have done with several bottles of wine, but settled for a Paris goblet, at one gulp, from the house carafe.

You tore up the bread with nervous fingers.

'Where were we?'

'It's not where I want to be.'

'It didn't feel like that when I held you.'

'No, you're right.'

'Well then?'

She has beautiful hands, I thought, watching her origami the baguette. Beautiful hands – deft, light, practical, practised. Mine was not the first body and it wouldn't be the last. She popped the bread into her mouth.

'Where shall I start?' I said, ready with my defence.

'Not at the beginning,' she said, feeding me crumbs.

'Why not?'

'We both know the usual reasons, the unwritten rules. No need to repeat them.'

'You really don't care, do you?'

'About you? Yes.'

'About the mess this will make.'

'I'm not a Virgo.'

'I am.'

'Oh God, just my luck. I bet you're obsessed with the laundry.'

'I am, as it happens.'

'Oh yes, I had a Virgo once. He could never leave the washing machine alone. Day and night, wash, wash, wash. I used to call him Lady Macbeth.'

'What are you going to call me?'

'I'll think of something.'

The artichoke arrived and I began to peel it away, fold by fold, layer by layer, dipping it. There is no secret about eating artichoke, or what the act resembles. Nothing else gives itself up so satisfyingly towards its centre. Nothing else promises and rewards. The tiny hairs are part of the pleasure.

What should I have eaten? Beetroot, I suppose.

A friend once warned me never to consider taking as a lover anyone who disliked either artichokes or champagne. That was good advice, but better advice might have been never to order artichokes or champagne with someone who should not be your lover.

At least I had chosen plain red wine.

And then I remembered the afternoon.

She looked at me, smiling, her lips glossy with oil.

'What are you thinking about?'

'This afternoon.'

'We should have gone to bed then.'

'We hardly spoke six sentences to each other.'

'That's the best way. Before the complications start.'

'Don't worry. No start. No complications.'

'Are you always such a moralist?'

'You make me sound like a Jehovah's Witness.'

'You can doorstep me any night.'

'Will you stop it?'

'As you say, we haven't started yet.'

'After supper we go back to the hotel and say goodnight.'

'And tomorrow you will catch the Eurostar to London.'

'And the day after you'll fly Air France to New York.'

'You must be a Jehovah's Witness.'

'Why must I?'

'You're not married but you won't sleep with me.'

'You are married.'

'That's my problem.'

'True …'

'Well then …'

'I've done it before and it became my problem.'

'What happened?'

'I fell in love.'

It was a long time ago. It feels like another life until I remember it was my life, like a letter you turn up in your own handwriting, hardly believing what it says.

I loved a woman who was married. She loved me too, and if there had been less love or less marriage I might have escaped. Perhaps no one really does escape.

She wanted me because I was a pool where she drank. I wanted her because she was a lover and a mother all mixed up into one. I wanted her because she was as beautiful as a warm afternoon with the sun on the rocks.

The damage done was colossal.

'You lost her?'

'Of course I did.'

'Have you got over it?'

'It was a love affair, not an assault course.'

'Love is an assault course.'

'Some wounds never heal.'

'I'm sorry.'

She held out her hand. What a strange world it is where you can have as much sex as you like but love is taboo. I'm talking about the real thing, the grand passion, which may not allow affection or convenience or happiness. The truth is that love smashes into your life like an ice floe, and even if your heart is built like the Titanic you go down. That's the size of it, the immensity of it. It's not proper, it's not clean, it's not containable.

She held out her hand. 'You're still angry.'

'I'm still alive.'

What to say? That the end of love is a haunting. A haunting of dreams. A haunting of silence. Haunted by ghosts, it is easy to become a ghost. Life ebbs. The pulse is too faint. Nothing stirs you. Some people approve of this and call it healing. It is not healing. A dead body feels no pain.

'But pain is pointless.'

'Not always.'

'Then what is the use of suffering? Can you tell me that?'

She thinks I'm holding on to pain. She thinks the pain is a souvenir. Perhaps she thinks that pain is the only way I can feel. As it is, the pain reminds me that my feelings are damaged. The pain doesn't stop me loving – only a false healing could do that – the pain tells me that neither my receptors nor my transmitters are in perfect working order. The pain is not feeling, but it has become an instrument of feeling.

She said, 'Do you still like having sex?'

'You talk as though I've had an amputation.'

'I think you have. I think someone has cut out your heart.'

———

I looked at her and my eyes were clear.

'That's not how the story ends.'

She put out her hand. 'I want to rescue you.'
    'From what?'
    'From the past. From pain.'
    'The past is only a way of talking.'
    'Then from pain.'
    'I don't want a wipe-clean life.'
    'Don't be so prickly.'
    'I'm sorry.'
    'What do you want? Tell me.'
    'No compromises.'
    'That's impossible.'
    'Only the impossible is worth the effort.'
    'Are you a fanatic or an idealist?'
    'Why do you need to label me?'
    'I need to understand.'
    'No, you want to explain me to yourself. You're not
sure, so you need a label. But I'm not a piece of furniture
with the price on the back.'
    'This is a heavy way to get some sex.'

The waitress cleared the plates and brought us some
brown and yellow banded ice cream, the same colour as
the ceilings and walls. It even had the varnishy look of the

1930s. The cherries round the edges were like Garbo kisses. You speared one and fed it to me.

'Come to bed with me.'

'Now?'

'Yes now. It's all I can offer. It's all I can ask.'

'No difficulties, no complications?'

'None.'

'Except that someone will be waiting for you in Room 29.'

'He'll be drunk and fast asleep.'

'And someone will be waiting for me.'

'Someone special?'

'Just a friend.'

'Well then ...'

'Good manners?'

'I'll leave a message at the night desk.'

She got up and fiddled with some change for the phone. 'Wait ...'

She didn't answer. There she was, at the phone, her face turned away from me.

We went to a small hotel that used to be a spa.

The bathrooms still have steam vents and needle showers, and if you turn the wrong knob while you're cleaning your teeth the whole bedroom will fill up with steam like the set of a Hitchcock movie. From somewhere out of the steam the phone will ring. There will be a footstep on the landing, voices. Meanwhile you'll be stumbling for the window, naked, blinded, with only a toothbrush between yourself and Paris.

The room we took at the Hotel Tonic was on the top floor. It had three beds with candlewick counterpanes and a view over the rooftops of the street. Opposite us, cut into the frame of the window, was a boy dancing alone to a Tina Turner record. We leaned out against the metal safety bars, watching him, watching the cars pull away. You put your hand on the small of my back under my shirt.

This is how we made love.

You kissed my throat.

    The boy was dancing.

    You kissed my collarbone.

    Two taxi drivers were arguing in the street.

    You put your tongue into the channel of my breasts.

    A door slammed underneath us.

    I opened your legs on to my hip.

    Two pigeons were asleep under the red wings of the roof.

    You began to move with me – hands, tongue, body.

    Game-show laughter from the television next door.

    You took my breasts in both hands and I slid you out of your jeans.

    Rattle of bottles on a tray.

    You don't wear knickers.

    A door opened. The tray was set down.

    You keep your breasts in a black mesh cage.

Car headlights reflected in the dressing-table mirror.

Lie down with me.

Get on top of me.

Ease yourself, just there, just there ...

Harry speaks French, he'll pick up the beer.

Push.

Stella or Bud?

Harder.

Do you want nuts?

Make me come. Make me.

Ring her after midnight your time, she said.

Just fuck me.

Got the number?

Fuck me.


The next morning I woke late and turned over to kiss her.

She had gone. The sheet was still warm but she had gone.

# Why Be Happy When You Could Be Normal?

*WHY BE HAPPY When You Could Be Normal?* was written in a jolt of energy. In two weeks I found I had 15,000 words.

   Why?

Is it a memoir? Not really. I think of it as an experiment with experience. None of us recalls our past as though we had carefully filmed it every moment of every day. And what if we had done? What lies beyond the frame? What was happening in our minds? There is always more to say, more to see, more to know.

I had a breakdown between summer 2007 and the end of 2008. In the autumn of 2008 someone I had loved deeply died too early, and at Christmas of that year my father died too. I buried him in a cold Saturnian January, and can-celled an interview with Susie Orbach, a woman I much admired and yet had never met. By May 2009 Susie and I were lovers.

And I had started to hunt for my birth mother – or Bio-Ma, as we called her.

Why?

Clearing out my father's things, I found some paperwork – yellowed, typewritten, as ancient as a codex, or so it felt, but really only from the early 1960s. My adoption. Some details about where I had been, and who I had been before that adoption.

I was no longer in breakdown, and Susie was, and is, a huge part of the healing of my mind. With her, I was able to go through the cellular trauma of looking into a past I had written (*Oranges Are Not The Only Fruit*) in order to own it, understand it, and, yes, to control it.

I knew early, how or why I don't know, that if you can read yourself as a fiction as well as a fact, you will be freer. If you are a story, you can change that story, especially how it ends.

I know this kind of thinking has been hijacked by the neo-liberal agenda of anyone can be a millionaire, a celebrity, a president. And if you are not what or who you want to be, it is your fault. Social justice and global inequality, class, race, background, has nothing to do with it. Utter crap and we know that.

But . . .

For some reason my imagination was strong and I was aligned with myself in crucial ways. For all the fuck-ups and failures, I knew I could write my way out – and I did.

*Oranges* is fiction. It's not the story of my life and I am not the Jeanette in that story. That is the point. I became my own fiction.

But . . .

Twenty-seven years after writing that book, the cluster of happenings I have described – and one I seem to have left out – forced me back towards the material I knew, and forward towards new material I never thought I wanted, or needed, to face.

As a writer I find I am forced towards discomfort, which is not the same thing as discontent.

The title comes from a Mrs W line, the day she gave me the clear choice of giving up the girl I loved or leaving home. I was sixteen. In our gloomy, cramped terraced house, with its body-count backyard (the kind of place where you bury your victims), and where she had operatically burnt my books in a Gotterdammerung of destruction, she asked me why I was doing this ('this' being in love, fatally, transgressively). I said, 'It makes me happy.' She said, 'WBHWYCBN?'

I wondered then, and have done for a long time since, whether this was a true binary, like black/white, good/evil, day/night, happy/normal?

It was a good question, if a brutal one, for us to end on. It was a gift, though a dark one, though I didn't know it at the time.

She was a violent philosopher.

WHEN LOVE IS UNRELIABLE and you are a child, you assume that it is the nature of love – its quality – to be unreliable. Children do not find fault with their parents until later. In the beginning the love you get is the love that sets.

I did not know that love could have continuity. I did not know that human love could be depended upon. Mrs Winterson's god was the God of the Old Testament and it may be that modelling yourself on a deity who demands absolute love from his 'children' but thinks nothing of drowning them (Noah's Ark), attempting to kill the ones who madden him (Moses), and letting Satan ruin the life of the most blameless of them all (Job), is bad for love.

True, God reforms himself and improves thanks to his relationship with human beings, but Mrs Winterson was not an interactive type; she didn't like human beings and she never did reform or improve. She was always striking me down, and then making a cake to put things right, and very often after a lockout we'd walk down to the fish and chip shop the next night and sit on the bench outside eating from the newspaper and watching people come and go.

For most of my life I have behaved in much the same way because that is what I learned about love. Add to that my own wildness and intensity and love becomes pretty

**When love is unreliable and you are a child, you assume that it is the nature of love – its quality – to be unreliable**

dangerous. I never did drugs, I did love — the crazy reckless kind, more damage than healing, more heartbreak than health. And I fought and hit out and tried to put it right the next day. And I went away without a word and didn't care.

Love is vivid. I never wanted the pale version. Love is full strength. I never wanted the diluted version. I never shied away from love's hugeness but I had no idea that love could be as reliable as the sun. The daily rising of love.

# The Gap of Time

THE GAP OF TIME is a cover version of Shakespeare's *The Winter's Tale*. It was commissioned by the Hogarth Press as part of their Shakespeare celebrations for the 400th anniversary of his death in 2016.

It never occurred to me to work with any other play; not because I don't know them and love them – probably I go back to Shakespeare more than any other writer – but because this one has so many personal connections. Or do I mean personal obsessions?

Time. Second Chances. Forgiveness. Love (always love). And . . .

At the shining centre of the play is an abandoned child. And I am.

As an adopted child, I was always trying to get a reading of myself. Foundling stories of every kind were signs, symbols, symmetries and clues. Often the child left to chance becomes the key to what happens next in the larger drama – but in non-linear time, 'next' can signify backwards as well as forwards. We imagine that the future depends on the past. In *The Winter's Tale* the past depends on the future. Time's arrow shoots both ways until that which is lost is found.

But time's not an arrow, is it?

Time is a boomerang.

The past keeps returning until we nail it.

My version of Shakespeare's story is set now. I didn't want Leontes to be King of Sicilia, but he had to be an Alpha Male who does what he likes, and who is reckless with the lives of others. So I made him a banker called Leo who runs Sicilia, a hedge fund. His wife, MiMi, is a singer, as a nod to the fact that the play itself is full of songs. Polixenes, Leontes's best friend and supposed seducer of Hermione (MiMi), becomes Xeno. Xeno is a gay man. A video-game designer living in New Bohemia, a fictional city in America, based on New Orleans.

In my story the two boys were sent to boarding school together by their divorcing families. This at least gives us a sense of their shared damage and shared experience.

Shakespeare gives us no back story to any of his characters in *The Winter's Tale*. We see a long friendship between two men, a possessive marriage, a jealous husband.

But we see, too, a friendship between Hermione and Polixenes that is intimate and playful. I wanted to preserve that friendship in my version – so I had Xeno sent by Leo to woo MiMi back to him after their first parting.

MiMi and Xeno find there is an attraction. Neither acts on it.

---

IT WAS AUGUST. THE banks of the Seine had been transformed into a seaside fantasy, part *plage*, part stalls of street food and pop-up bars. The weather was hot. People were easy.

Leo had sent Xeno to ask MiMi to give him another chance.

'I'll mess it up if I see her. You explain.'

'What do you want me to say?'

'I don't know! The long form of "I love you."'

Leo gave Xeno a piece of paper in his bad handwriting. 'This is the long form.'

Xeno looked at it. He nearly laughed, but his friend was so hangdog and anxious that he just nodded while he was reading.

'I've been working on it,' said Leo.

1  Can I live without you? Yes.

2  Do I want to? No.

3  Do I think about you often? Yes.

4  Do I miss you? Yes.

5  Do I think about you when I am with another woman? Yes.

6  Do I think that you are different to other women? Yes.

7   Do I think that I am different to other men? No.

8   Is it about sex? Yes.

9   Is it only about sex? No.

10   Have I felt like this before? Yes and no.

11   Have I felt like this since you? No.

12   Why do I want to marry you? I hate the idea of
      you marrying someone else.

13   You are beautiful.

So when they had walked awhile and stopped for water at
a bar selling *l'eau* in fancy blue bottles, Xeno got out the
piece of paper and gave it to MiMi. She started laughing. 'No,
listen,' said Xeno, 'he's awkward but he means it. This is his
way of being sure.'

MiMi shook her head. 'I don't know.'

'Then say yes,' said Xeno.

'Pourquoi?'

They walked on. They talked about life as flow. About noth-
ingness. About illusion. About love as a theory marred by
practice. About love as practice marred by theory. They
talked about the impossibility of sex. Was sex different for
men? With men? What did it feel like to fall in love? To fall
out of love?

'There's a theory,' said Xeno, 'the Gnostics started it as
a rival to Christianity right back at the start; this world,
ours, was created Fallen, not by God, who is absent, but by

a Lucifer-type figure. Some kind of dark angel. We didn't sin, or fall from grace, it wasn't our fault. We were born this way. Everything we do is falling. Even walking is a kind of controlled falling. But that's not the same as failing. And if we know this (gnosis) the pain is easier to bear.'

'The pain of love?'

'What else is there? Love. Lack of love. Loss of love. I never bought into status and power – even fear of death – as independent drivers. The platform we stand on, or fall from, is love.'

'That is romantic for a man who never commits.'

'I like the idea,' said Xeno. 'But I like the idea of living on the moon too. Sadly, it's 293,000 miles away and has no water.'

'But you have come here to see me because you want me to marry Leo.'

'I'm just the messenger.'

They walked to a restaurant in a triangle where some boys were playing boules. A man was exercising two Dalmatians, throwing a red tennis ball. Black and white and red. Black and white and red. The evening was cooling.

They ordered artichokes and haddock. Xeno sat beside MiMi while she talked him through the menu.

'What about you?' MiMi asked Xeno.

'I'm moving to America – the gaming work is there.'

'But you'll be around?'

'I'll always be around.'

**What else is there? Love. Lack of love. Loss of love. I never bought into status and power – even fear of death – as independent drivers. The platform we stand on, or fall from, is love**

What would it be like if we didn't have a body? If we communicated as spirits do? Then I wouldn't notice the smile of you, the curve of you, *the hair that falls into your eyes,* your arms on the table, brown with faint hairs, *the way you hook your boots on the bar of the chair,* that my eyes are grey and yours are green, *that your eyes are grey and mine are green,* that you have a crooked mouth, that you are petite but your legs are long like a sentence I can't finish, *that your hands are sensitive, and the way you sit close to me to read the menu so that I can explain what things are in French,* and I love your accent, the way you speak English, and never before has anyone said "addock' the way you say it, and it is no longer a smoked fish but a word that sounds like (the word that comes to mind and is dismissed is love). *Do you always leave your top button undone like that? Just one button? So that I can imagine your chest from the animal paw of hair that I can see?* She's not a blonde. No. I think her hair is naturally dark but I like the way she colours it in sections and the way she slips off her shoes under the table. Disconcerting, the way you look at me when we talk. *What were we talking about?*

She ordered a baba au rhum and the waiter brought the St James rum in a bottle and plonked it on the table.

She said, 'Sometimes I'm Hemingway: I I am a Chamberry kir with oysters. Later, for inspiration, a rum St James. It's a brute.'

Xeno sniffed it. Barbecue fuel. But he poured a shot anyway.

She drank her coffee. A couple walked by fighting about the dry-cleaning. You meet someone and you can't wait to get your clothes off. A year later and you're fighting about the dry-cleaning. The imperfections are built into the design.

But then, thought Xeno, beauty isn't beauty because it's perfect.

MiMi was sitting with her knees up, bare legs, her eyes like fireflies.

Xeno smiled: what was number 13 on Leo's list? *You are beautiful.*

They walked hand in hand back to the apartment on Saint Julien le Pauvre.

The staircase was dark. Xeno ran his hand up the seventeenth century iron banister that curved up the building as the narrow staircase rounded the landings like a recurring dream and the doors were closed onto other rooms.

MiMi opened the door into her apartment. The only light came from the street lamps outside. She hadn't closed the long shutters. She went over to the window, standing framed in the window in her blue dress in the yellow light, like a Matisse cut-out of herself.

Xeno came and stood behind her. He didn't shut the front door and he had such a quiet way of moving that she seemed not to hear him. He wondered what she was thinking.

He was directly behind her now. She smelled of limes and mint. She turned. She turned right into Xeno. Up against him. He put his arms round her and she rested her head on his chest.

For a moment they stood like that, then MiMi took his hand and led him to her bed – a big *bateau lit* in the back of the apartment. She lifted her hand and stroked the nape of his neck.

On the landing outside, the electric light, footsteps up the stairs, a woman's heavy French accent complaining about the hot weather. A man grunting in response. The couple climbed slowly on past MiMi's apartment, carrying their groceries, not even glancing in through the open door.

And then Xeno was walking swiftly down the stairs.

Inside *The Winter's Tale* are stories embryonic and untold. On the stage it isn't possible to run those multiple stories. The action and drama must move forward in the two hours or so of theatre.

In a novel it's possible to lift those buried stories into view. The form lends itself to interiority and reflection. We get a glimpse of something and we follow it in our minds.

But the drama still has to happen – and the speed at which *The Winter's Tale* hits us – like an out-of-control truck – was what I wanted for the opening of the novel. So I inverted the structure of the play so that the opening chapter blasts us straight into a car-jack and murder, one stormy night in New Bohemia. And suddenly there's an abandoned baby left in a hospital BabyHatch.

Shakespeare has Perdita, 'the little lost one', raised by a Shepherd and his son the Clown. For me, Shep and Clo are a couple of late-night black guys who instinctively do the right thing at the right time.

For Shakespeare, recognising time as a player is central to so much of his work. There's a time to get things right – or disastrously wrong. Leontes – because he doesn't understand that he doesn't own time – learns the hard way. Shakespeare's late plays are about second chances and forgiveness. As I get older both things matter to me more. I'm an optimist but time is short. Getting things wrong is easier than getting things right. I'm aware of how much we need the generosity and patience of others.

In *The Winter's Tale*, it's the women, Hermione, Perdita and Paulina, who pull the thing to rights. They are an interesting manifestation of the Great Goddess in her triple form as mother, daughter and wise woman. The female principle saves the play from the usual consequences of male rage.

And at last, in Shakespeare, the women stop dying in the fall-out of the hero's soul. Hermione, Perdita and Paulina are alive at the end of *The Winter's Tale*. That's progress.

If there are only four possible endings to any story – comedy, tragedy, revenge and forgiveness – then Shakespeare leaves us where we want to be, as the motionless statue of Hermione steps down to rejoin the flow of time, and to let the past be over.

I altered the ending because I wanted the last word to be Perdita's. If the future exists, the new generation will have to discover it, like a territory not subject to the violent destructiveness of the past.

It has been strange, in the middle of so much global horror, to work with this play. Shakespeare had had it with the 'Great Man' theory of history. The heroes and villains are done. Instead, almost shyly, the women are on stage and the baby – nearly destroyed but saved – has returned.

Here's the very last part of the book:

## PERDITA

SOON THIS WILL become our life together and we have to live in the world like everyone else. We have to go to work, have children, make homes, make dinner, make love, and the world is low on goodness these days so our lives may come to nothing. We will have dreams but will they come true?

Maybe we'll forget that we were the site where the miracle happened. The place of pilgrimage that fell into disuse, overgrown with weeds, run-down and neglected. Maybe we won't stay together. Maybe life is too hard anyway. Maybe love is just for the movies.

Maybe we'll hurt each other so much that we will deny that what happened happened. We'll find an alibi to prove that we were never there. Those people didn't exist.

Maybe, one night, when the weather is bad and you are holding my wrists too tight, I'll take a torch and go for a walk in the rain, my collar up against the wind, and the stars not there in the dark, and a bird startles out of the hedge, and there's the gleam of puddles under battery-light, and further off the sound of the main road, but here the sound of the night and my footsteps and my breathing.

Maybe then I will remember that, although history repeats itself and we always fall, and I am a carrier of history whose brief excursion into time leaves no mark, yet I have known something worth knowing, wild and unlikely and against every rote.

Like a pocket of air in an upturned boat.

Love. The size of it. The scale of it. Unimaginable. Vast. Your love for me. My love for you. Our love for one another. Real. Yes. Though I find my way by flashlight in the dark, I am witness and evidence of what I know; this love.

The atom and jot of my span.

# Christmas Days

WHY ARE THE REAL things, the important things, so easily mislaid under the things that hardly matter at all?

When I was having a breakdown I came home one night to a cold, empty house and I was too depressed to cook or light the fire. And too broken to sleep.

Christmas was coming and so I decided to tell myself a story.

I learned this years ago, as a child, when my mother, Mrs Winterson, used to shut me in the coal-shed as a punishment.

There are only two things you can do when locked in a coal-shed: count coal, a limited activity, or tell yourself a story. And so I escaped my confinement as many have done before me – by vanishing into my imagination.

———

That Christmas, then, I thought I would re-tell the Nativity story from the point of view of the Donkey. Nothing special about that, except that I was the Donkey, feeling small, overlooked, unlikely, carrying my own body weight and too much more. In the story the Donkey auditions with all the animals for the job of carrying the Christ Child. Down to the last three, he has to beat the Lion: '*If He is to be the King of the World, He should be carried by the King of the Beasts.*' And the Unicorn: '*If He is to be the Mystery of the World, He should be carried by the most mysterious of us all.*'

The Donkey says, '*If He is to bear the Burdens of the World, He had better be carried by me . . .*'

Later in the story, the angels are sitting on the wormy, shattered roof of the stable, their feet dangling over the rim of time. A foot touches the Donkey's nose, and it turns golden.

I had need of a golden nose.

The twelve stories in the collection are mixed up with twelve recipes. These recipes, like Ruth Rendell's Red Cabbage or Kamila Shamsie's Turkey Biriyani, are all food cooked with friends, or personal rituals, like My New Year's Day Steak Sandwich.

I put in everything I like. Christmas doesn't have to be a commercial hijack, but the only way to prevent that is to make it personal and meaningful.

Our lives are losing both the personal and the

meaningful. Every occasion to return those values matters. And Christmas is celebrated all over the world by people of faith and people of no faith. It is potentially a time for coming together, as well as a time for reflection.

And, in these dark days of nationalism and unthinking hatreds, community and reflection give us a different world view. One planet. One people. Many different lives.

The book is a celebration of Christmas and a history of Christmas. Here are the myths and facts of Christmas: did you know it was the Coca-Cola Company that gave Santa a makeover in 1931, and turned his green robes red?

Did you know that Puritans in England and New England succeeded in banning Christmas for years because it was too pagan?

You did? Well, just enjoy the stories, then: ghost stories, magical interventions, SnowMamas, speaking frogs and froglissimos, funny stories, spooky stories and love stories, of course. Because everything comes back to love.

TIME IS A BOOMERANG, not an arrow.

I was adopted by Pentecostals and stamped Missionary. Christmas was important in the missionary calendar. From the beginning of November, either we were preparing packages to send to the Foreign Field or we were preparing packages to deliver to those in Hot Places returning to the Home Front.

It might have been because my parents had been in

WWII. It might have been because we lived in End Time, waiting for Armageddon. Whatever the reason, there was a drill to Christmas, from making the mincemeat for the mince pies to singing carols to, or rather at, the unsaved of Accrington. Still, Mrs Winterson loved Christmas. It was the one time of the year when she went out into the world looking as though the world was more than a vale of tears.

She was an unhappy woman, and so this happy time in our house was precious. I am sure I love Christmas because she did.

On December 21st every year my mother went out in her hat and coat while my father and I strung up the paper chains, made by me, from the corners of the parlour cornice to the centre light bulb.

Eventually my mother returned, in what seemed to be a hailstorm, though maybe that was her personal weather. She carried a goose, half-in, half-out of her shopping bag, its slack head hung sideways like a dream nobody can remember. She passed it to me – goose and dream – and I plucked the feathers into a bucket. We kept the feathers to restuff whatever needed restuffing, and we saved the thick goose fat drained from the bird for roasting potatoes through the winter. Apart from Mrs W, who had a thyroid problem, everyone we knew was as thin as a ferret. We needed goose fat.

After I had left home, and later gone to university at Oxford, I went back to the old house, that first Christmastime. My mother had given me the ultimatum to leave home long since, when I fell in love with a girl, and in a religious house like ours I might as well have married a goat. We hadn't spoken since that time. I had lived in a Mini for a bit, lodged with a teacher and eventually left town.

During my first term at Oxford I received a postcard – one of those postcards that says POST CARD in blue letters at the top. Underneath, in her immaculate copperplate handwriting, was the message: ARE YOU COMING HOME THIS CHRISTMAS? LOVE MOTHER.

As I reached our little terraced house at the top of the street I could hear the mostly musical sounds of what is best described as a bossa-nova version of 'In the Bleak Midwinter'. My mother had thrown out the old upright piano and got herself an electronic organ with double keyboard, orchestra stops, drum and bass.

She hadn't seen me for two years. Nothing was said. We spent the next hour admiring the effects of snare drum and trumpet solo on 'Hark! The Herald Angels Sing'.

My Oxford friend from St Lucia was due to visit me at home, which was brave of her, but when I had tried to explain about my family she thought I was exaggerating.

At first the visit was a great success. Mrs W considered a black friend as a missionary endeavour all of its own. She went round to the retired missionaries from the church and asked, 'What do they eat?' Pineapples, came the answer.

When Vicky arrived my mother gave her a wool blanket

she had knitted so that Vicky would not be cold. 'They feel the cold,' she told me.

Mrs Winterson was an obsessive and she had been knitting for Jesus all year. The Christmas tree had knitted decorations on it, and the dog was imprisoned inside a Christmas coat of red wool with white snowflakes. There was a knitted Nativity scene, and the shepherds were wearing little scarves because this was Bethlehem on the bus route to Accrington.

My dad opened the door dressed in a knitted waistcoat and matching knitted tie. The whole house had been re-knitted.

Mrs W was in a merry mood. 'Would you like some gammon and pineapple, Vicky? Cheese on toast with pineapple? Pineapples and cream? Pineapple upside-down cake? Pineapple fritters?'

Eventually, after a few days of this fare, Vicky said, 'I don't like pineapple.'

Mrs W's mood changed at once. She didn't speak to us for the rest of the day and she crushed up a papier-mâché robin. The next morning, at breakfast, the table was set with a pyramid of unopened tins of pineapple chunks and a Victorian postcard of two cats on their hind legs dressed up like Mr and Mrs. The caption said NOBODY LOVES US.

That night, when Vicky went to bed, she found that her pillow had been taken out of its pillowcase, and the pillowcase stuffed with warning leaflets about the Apocalypse.

She wondered whether to go home, but I'd seen worse and I thought things might improve.

On Christmas Eve we had a group of carol singers round from the church. Mrs W did seem happier. She had forced me and Vicky to wrap several half-cabbages in tinfoil and spear them with cocktail sticks of Cheddar cheese, topped with the rejected pineapple chunks.

She called these things sputniks. It was something to do with the Cold War. Tinfoil? Antennae? The scaremongering that the KGB had listening devices hidden in cheese?

Never mind. The offending pineapples had found a purpose and we were all singing carols quite happily when there was a knock at the door. It turned out to be the Salvation Army singing carols too.

This was reasonable. It was Christmas-time. But Mrs Winterson was having none of it. She opened the front door and shouted, 'Jesus is here. Go away.'

Slam.

When I went away after that Christmas I never went back. I never saw Mrs W again – she was soon too furious about my debut novel, *Oranges Are Not The Only Fruit*. Quote: 'It's the first time I've had to order a book in a false name.'

She died in 1990.

As you get older you remember the dead at Christmas. The Celts, during their midwinter festival of Samhain, expected the dead to join the living. Many cultures would understand that; not ours.

That is a pity. And a loss. If time is a boomerang and not an arrow, then the past is always returning and repeating. Memory, as a creative act, allows us to reawaken the dead, or sometimes to lay them to rest, as at last we understand our past.

Last Christmas I was alone in my kitchen, the fire lit — I love having a fire in the kitchen. I was pouring myself a drink when Judy Garland came on the radio singing 'Have Yourself a Merry Little Christmas'. I remembered how Mrs W had played that song on the piano. It was one of those moments we all know, of sadness and sweetness mixed together. Regret? Yes, I think so, for everything we got wrong. But recognition too, because she was a remarkable woman. She deserved a miracle to get her out of her trapped life of no hope, no money, no possibility of change.

Fortunately, she got the miracle. Unfortunately, the miracle was me. I was the Golden Ticket. I could have taken her anywhere. She could have been free ...

The Christmas story of the Christ Child is complex. Here's what it tells us about miracles:

Miracles are never convenient (the baby's going to be born whether or not there's a hotel room — and there isn't).

Miracles are not what we expect (an obscure man and woman find themselves parenting the Saviour of the World).

Miracles detonate the existing situation — and the blow-up and the back-blast mean some people get hurt.

What is a miracle? A miracle is an intervention – it breaks through the space-time continuum. A miracle is an intervention that cannot be accounted for purely rationally. Chance and fate are in the mix. A miracle is a benign intervention, yes, but miracles are like the genie in the bottle – let them out and there's a riot. You'll get your Three Wishes, but a whole lot else besides.

Mrs W wanted a baby. She couldn't have one. Along comes me – but as she often said, 'The Devil led us to the wrong crib.' Satan as a faulty star.

That's the fairy-tale element of the story.

Sometimes the thing we long for, the thing we need, the miracle we want, is right there in front of us, and we can't see it, or we run the other way, or, saddest of all, we just don't know what to do with it. Think how many people get the success they want, the partner they want, the money they want, et cetera, and turn it into dust and ashes – like the fairy gold no one can spend.

So at Christmas I think about the Christmas story, and all the Christmas stories since. As a writer I know that we get along badly without space in our lives for imagination and reflection. Religious festivals were designed to be time outside of time. Time where ordinary time was subject to significant time. What we remember. What we invent.

So light a candle to the dead.

And light a candle to miracles, however unlikely, and pray that you recognise yours.

And light a candle to the living; the world of friendship and family that means so much.

And light a candle to the future; that it may happen and not be swallowed up by darkness.

And light a candle to love.

Lucky Love.

# Afterword

LOVE – THAT moves the sun and the other stars? As Dante put it?

Love is as strong as death – as the Bible puts it.

Or this: 'When my love swears that she is made of truth/I do believe her, though I know she lies.' (WS. SONNET 138)

So many versions of love. So many love songs. So much that is romantic. Or sentimental.

I am still looking for clues. Still trying to understand what should be obvious, and isn't: how to love.

How to love?

Experience. Heartbreak. But hearts are made to be broken. It's integral to the design.

Writing is the best way I know to talk about the most difficult thing I know: Love.

THE DOOR OF the house opens. It's you, coming out of the house, coming towards me, smiling, pleased. It's you, and it's me, and I knew it would end like this, that you would be there, had always been there; it was just a matter of time.

Everything is imprinted forever with what it once was.

JEANETTE WINTERSON OBE was born in Manchester. Adopted by Pentecostal parents, she was raised to be a missionary. This did and didn't work out.

Discovering early the power of books, she left home at 16 to live in a Mini and get on with her education. After graduating from Oxford University she worked for a while in the theatre and published her first novel at 25. *Oranges Are Not The Only Fruit* is based on her own upbringing but using herself as a fictional character. She scripted the novel into a BAFTA-winning BBC drama. 27 years later she revisited that material in the bestselling memoir *Why Be Happy When You Could Be Normal?* She has written 10 novels for adults, as well as children's books, non-fiction and screenplays. She writes regularly for the *Guardian*. She lives in the Cotswolds in a wood and in Spitalfields, London.

She believes that art is for everyone and it is her mission to prove it.

RECOMMENDED BOOKS BY JEANETTE WINTERSON:

*Oranges Are Not The Only Fruit*
*Why Be Happy When You Could Be Normal?*
*Christmas Days*

BOOKS BY JEANETTE WINTERSON

Novels
*Oranges Are Not The Only Fruit*
*The Passion*
*Sexing the Cherry*
*Written on the Body*
*Art and Lies*
*Gut Symmetries*
*The Powerbook*
*Lighthousekeeping*
*The Stone Gods*
*The Gap of Time*

Comic Book
*Boating for Beginners*

Short Stories
*The World and Other Places*
*Midsummer Nights (ed.)*
*Christmas Days*

Novellas
*Weight (Myth)*
*The Daylight Gate (Horror)*

Non-fiction
*Art Objects: Essays in Ecstasy and Effrontery*

Memoir
*Why Be Happy When You Could Be Normal?*

Collaboration
*LAND (with Antony Gormley and Clare Richardson)*

Children's Books
*Tanglewreck*
*The Lion, the Unicorn and Me*
*The King of Capri*
*The Battle of the Sun*

# How do we express Love?

Eating
NIGELLA LAWSON

VINTAGE MINIS

Jealousy
MARCEL PROUST

VINTAGE MINIS

Babies
ANNE ENRIGHT

VINTAGE MINIS

Desire
HARUKI MURAKAMI

VINTAGE MINIS

## VINTAGE MINIS

The Vintage Minis bring you the world's greatest writers on the experiences that make us human. These stylish, entertaining little books explore the whole spectrum of life – from birth to death, and everything in between. Which means there's something here for everyone, whatever your story.

vintageminis.co.uk